Oliver Twist

Oliver Twist

CHARLES DICKENS

Illustrated by CHRISTIAN BIRMINGHAM

Abridged from the original by LESLEY BAXTER

With an introduction by MICHAEL MORPURGO

HarperCollins *Children's Books*

First published in Great Britain
by HarperCollins Publishers Ltd in 1996.

This edition published
by HarperCollins Children's Books in 2012

1 3 5 7 9 10 8 6 4 2

ISBN: 978-0-00-746377-0

HarperCollins Children's Books is a division
of HarperCollins Publishers Ltd.

Illustrations copyright © Christian Birmingham 1996
Abridgement copyright © Lesley Baxter 1996
Introduction copyright © Michael Morpurgo 1996

The illustrator and authors reserve the moral right to be identified
as the illustrator and authors of this work.

Visit our website at www.harpercollins.co.uk

Printed and bound in China

INTRODUCTION

Like so many children during the last hundred years, I grew up with *Oliver Twist*. I think I must have seen the film first. Then I read the book surreptitiously, under my blankets with a torch, not the real thing of course, but an edition called "Classics Illustrated" – a comic strip version. (We weren't allowed to read comics.) Later on, much later on, I read the book itself, with the Cruikshank illustrations. Then came the Lionel Bart musical, and after that the film of the musical.

As a young teacher I found myself not only "teaching" *Oliver Twist*, but producing a school performance of the musical. That was when I began singing "Oliver" in my bath. What is it about a bath that makes me sound so much like Pavarotti? There was "Food, Glorious Food", or "You've Got to Pick a Pocket or Two", and every time I sang them I would go back in my mind's eye to the story that inspired them.

There can hardly be a story in the English language more widely known, nor more dearly loved than *Oliver Twist*. Now why should that be? After all, it is set in a time and place both very far removed from our own. The language of Charles Dickens is most certainly not easily accessible to a modern reader. His sentences are long, and often complex in construction. Most of his vocabulary has fallen into disuse and become antique. All this must surely have a distancing effect for us today. But somehow it doesn't. We read on avidly, because *Oliver Twist* is a rattling good yarn, a page-turner that touches the human spirit no matter when or where we live.

It is not only the language, though, that might be a problem to a modern reader. There is the plot too. At best the plot is somewhat contrived; at worst it is a tissue of unlikely coincidences. Yet whilst we are reading it, we believe in it absolutely. That is the mark of a true magician, and Charles Dickens was just that. Many of the characters, such as Bill Sikes, Fagin, and Mr Brownlow, have often been said to be overdrawn, to be caricatures almost. But when we are deep in the book, they all seem utterly credible and convincing. You could say that the ending is predictable, and even a little trite. Yet it is the ending we all yearn for. There could be no other ending.

There is a temptation with all Dickens' novels to be comforted by the distance in time between his world and ours. After reading *A Christmas Carol* it is too easy to convince ourselves that all that overweening greed, all that abject poverty, was then, not now. We so easily say to ourselves: "Yes, but things aren't like that any more." So with *Oliver Twist*. Certainly our inner-city squalour today is not the squalour of Dickens' time, but it is squalour all the same. We do not have workhouses any more, but there are still young children on our streets, growing up among criminals, their young lives corrupted and twisted, and they are led, often irretrievably, into evil.

Oliver's triumph, the triumph of innocence over evil, would never have happened without Mr Brownlow. His kind are still needed, and will always be needed. Dickens' triumph is to have written a story so powerful, so universal, so true that we can learn as much from it now as his readers did in his lifetime. We journey with Oliver from his birth, through a terrifying labyrinth of fear and isolation. We are with him when he faces abuse and hunger and misery in the workhouse. We escape with him as he runs off to London, to something better, we hope, only to find him sucked into the dark and murky world of Fagin's den. We witness the twists and turns of fate, that take poor Oliver from deepest despair to soaring hope, and then down into despair again, before he emerges at last into the bright warmth of a loving home. All through it, we long to call out to him, to warn him, to protect him. But all we can do is be there with him, hold his hand, and hope he'll come through. He touches us as no other child in fiction. But we are also touched even by Fagin, in spite of all he does, and by Nancy too, and the ever cocky Artful Dodger – just as Oliver is. Only Bill Sikes, the epitome of cruelty and evil, is irredeemably beyond our sympathy, and Oliver's.

Dickens, ever the great communicator, would have relished the idea of a version of *Oliver Twist* especially for young people, and one so wonderfully illustrated too. No writer ever spoke more directly to his readers. It is no accident that his novels were so profusely illustrated, and that he read them in public as often as he did. He wanted his stories to be as widely read as possible. This edition will bring many children of today to *Oliver Twist* for the very first time, and they won't have to read it under the blankets with a torch either. For this is a taste of the real thing, a taste that will, I know, give them an appetite for more.

Charles Dickens himself said of *Oliver Twist* that he attempted "a something which was needed, and which would be a service to society. And I did it as best I could."

I can only add: "the best anyone could."

Michael Morpurgo
1996

CHAPTER 1

Oliver Twist was born in a workhouse for the poor and homeless. He lay gasping on a little mattress, and neither the surgeon nor the old pauper woman who ushered him into this world expected him to survive. Then, after a few struggles, he breathed, sneezed, and set up a loud cry. As he did so, his young mother raised her pale face from the pillow. "Let me see the child," she said faintly. The surgeon placed Oliver in his mother's arms. She held her son and tenderly kissed his forehead. . . Then she lay back, and died.

"It's all over, Mrs Thingummy," said the surgeon as he got ready to leave. "The child is weak and will very likely be troublesome. Give it a little gruel if it is." He put on his hat, and pausing by the bedside, added, "She was a good-looking girl. Where did she come from?"

"She was brought here last night," replied the old nurse. "She was found lying in the street. Where she came from, or where she was going to, nobody knows."

The surgeon leaned over the body, and raised the left hand. "No wedding ring, I see. Ah! Good night!"

The surgeon left and the nurse sat down by the fire and wrapped Oliver in a blanket. To look at, he could have been the child of a nobleman or a beggar, but it no longer mattered. Now he was the orphan of a workhouse.

Oliver was kept at the workhouse for eight or ten months, but no one could be found to look after him. He was sent to a branch workhouse nearby, where, with twenty or thirty other poor children, he was brought up by an elderly woman called Mrs Mann. She gave them the smallest possible portions of the weakest possible food, and barely enough clothes to keep them warm. In eight and a half cases out of ten, the children sickened from want and cold, or fell into the fire from neglect. Oliver grew up pale and thin, and by the time he reached his ninth birthday he was decidedly small for his age.

Oliver was spending his birthday locked in the cellar for presuming to be hungry, when Mrs Mann was unexpectedly startled by Mr Bumble, the beadle, striving to open the garden gate. Mr Bumble was a fat man, and short-tempered. He shook the gate, then he kicked it. Mrs Mann hurried out to meet him. Mr Bumble always made her nervous. She unbolted the gate and led him up to the house and into a small parlour, where she placed a seat for him and carefully set his hat and cane on the table.

"I shall come straight to my business," said the beadle. "Oliver Twist is nine years old today. We have never been able to find out who his father is, or what his mother's name was."

Mrs Mann thought for a moment, and then said, "How come he has any name at all, then?"

"I invented it," said Mr Bumble proudly. "We name our orphans in alphabetical order. The last was a S – Swubble, I called him. This one was a T – so I named him Twist. But he's too old to stay here. It's time he came back to the workhouse and earned a living."

"I'll fetch him directly," said Mrs Mann, and left the room.

She scrubbed Oliver's face and hands clean of dirt from the cellar, so as to impress the beadle, and led him into the parlour. He bowed to Mr Bumble, and then with a slice of bread in his hand and a little brown cloth cap on his head, he followed the beadle out of the house.

Mr Bumble walked with long strides; Oliver, firmly grasping the beadle's gold-laced cuff, trotted beside him, inquiring every so often whether they were "nearly there". Mr Bumble returned very brief and snappish replies.

Oliver had not been within the walls of the workhouse a quarter of an hour, and had scarcely demolished a second slice of bread, when Mr Bumble told him that he was to appear before the "board". Mr Bumble then gave him a tap on the head with his cane and led him into a large, whitewashed room, where eight fat gentlemen sat around a table. At the head of the table, seated in a chair higher than the rest, was a particularly fat gentleman with a very round, red face.

"What's your name, boy?" asked the gentleman.

Oliver was frightened at the sight of so many gentlemen, and the beadle gave him another tap with his cane, which made him jump. He answered in a very quiet voice, whereupon a gentleman in a white waistcoat said he was a fool.

"Boy," said the gentleman in the high chair, "you know you're an orphan, I suppose?"

"What's that, sir?" asked Oliver.

"The boy *is* a fool – I thought he was," said the gentleman in the white waistcoat.

"Hush!" said the gentleman who had spoken first. "You know you've got no father or mother, don't you?"

"Yes, sir," replied Oliver.

"Well, you have come here to be educated and taught a useful trade," said the red-faced gentleman in the high chair.

"So you'll start work tomorrow morning at six o'clock, making string from old rope," added the man in the white waistcoat.

Oliver bowed low to the gentlemen and was then hurried away to a large dormitory, where on a rough, hard bed he sobbed himself to sleep.

In the workhouse, Oliver was hungrier than he had ever been with Mrs Mann. Along with the other boys, he was given three meals of thin gruel a day, with an onion twice a week, and half a roll on Sundays.

The room in which he and his companions were fed was a large stone hall, with a copper pot at one end, out of which the master served one ladle of gruel to each boy. The bowls never wanted washing. The boys polished them with their spoons till they shone, then licked their fingers and stared hungrily at the pot.

The boys suffered the tortures of slow starvation for three months. At last they were so hungry that one of them hinted darkly that unless he had another bowl of gruel a day, he might eat the boy who slept next to him. The others believed him. Lots were cast to decide who should walk up to the master after supper that evening and ask for more; and it fell to Oliver Twist.

When evening arrived, the boys took their places. The master, in his cook's uniform, stationed himself at the pot. The gruel was served out, and disappeared. The boys whispered to each other and winked at Oliver; his neighbours nudged him. Oliver got up from the table, and advancing to the master, bowl and spoon in hand, said:

"Please, sir, I want some more."

The master was a fat, healthy man, but he turned very pale.

"What!" he said in a faint voice.

"Please, sir," replied Oliver, "I want some more."

The master aimed a blow at Oliver's head with the ladle and shrieked aloud for the beadle.

Mr Bumble arrived, and on hearing the news, rushed to the boardroom in great excitement. Addressing the gentleman in the high chair, he said, "Mr Limbkins, I beg your pardon, sir! Oliver Twist has asked for more!"

"For *more*!" said Mr Limbkins.

"That boy will be hung," said the gentleman in the white waistcoat. "I know that boy will be hung."

Oliver was taken to a dark room and locked inside. The next morning a notice was posted on the gates outside the workhouse. It offered five pounds to anyone who would take him away and put him to work.

Oliver stayed locked in the room for a week, until one morning when Mr Sowerberry the undertaker arrived at the workhouse.

"Please, sir, I want some more."

"You don't know anyone who wants a boy, do you?" Mr Bumble asked the undertaker. As he spoke he lifted his cane to the notice and gave three distinct raps upon the words "five pounds", which were written in very large capitals.

Mr Sowerberry thought for a while and then said, "Well, Mr Bumble, I think I'll take the boy myself."

So that evening Mr Bumble took Oliver to the undertaker's house. Tears slid down Oliver's cheeks as he was led through the streets, and even Mr Bumble felt a twinge of pity. He coughed two or three times to cover his embarrassment, then told Oliver to dry his eyes and be a good boy.

Mr Sowerberry had just closed his shop when Mr Bumble and Oliver arrived. The undertaker called to his wife. "My dear," said Mr Sowerberry, "this is the boy from the workhouse that I told you of."

"Dear me!" said the undertaker's wife. "He's very small."

"He *is* rather small," said Mr Bumble. "But he'll grow, Mrs Sowerberry. He'll grow."

Mrs Sowerberry sniffed. "I daresay he will," she replied. "But it will be us that will be feeding him!" And with that she opened a side door and pushed Oliver down a steep flight of stairs into the damp, dark kitchen. There Oliver was given the remains of the dinner that had been left for Trip the dog. Afterwards Mrs Sowerberry took a dim and dirty lamp and led the way upstairs again.

"Your bed's under the counter," she said to Oliver. "You don't mind sleeping among the coffins, I suppose?"

Oliver dared not protest. That night he slept amongst the shadows of the shop, half expecting to see some frightful form slowly rear its head from one of the coffins that stood in the middle of the room.

He was awakened in the morning by a loud kicking at the shop door.

"Open the door, will yer?" cried a voice through the keyhole.

Oliver unbolted the door.

"I beg your pardon, sir," Oliver said, seeing a large, fierce-looking boy. "Did you want a coffin?"

"You'll be needin' one before long," said the boy, and he entered the shop, kicking Oliver as he went. He had a large head and very small eyes. "I'm Mister Noah Claypole, and you're under me. Take down the shutters!"

Oliver took down the shutters, and broke a pane of glass in his efforts to stagger away beneath the weight of the first one. Noah, having assured Oliver he would "catch it", condescended to help him with the rest. Mr Sowerberry came down shortly after, and soon Mrs Sowerberry appeared. Oliver "caught it" as Noah had predicted, for Mr Sowerberry boxed his ears. Then Oliver followed Noah downstairs for breakfast.

"Come near the fire, Noah," said Charlotte, the housemaid. "I saved a nice bit of bacon for you from master's breakfast." Meanwhile, Oliver sat shivering on a box in the coldest corner of the room, and ate the stale pieces which had been specially reserved for him.

Oliver had been with the undertaker for some three weeks or a month. Mr and Mrs Sowerberry were taking their supper in the little back-parlour when the undertaker, after several glances at his wife, said, "My dear, I want to ask your advice. It's about young Twist. A very good-looking boy, that, my dear."

"He ought to be, he eats enough," observed Mrs Sowerberry.

"There's a look of sadness in his face," continued Mr Sowerberry, "which is very appealing. He would make a delightful mute, my dear."

Mrs Sowerberry looked up with an expression of wonderment.

"I don't mean a regular mute to attend grown-up people, my dear,"

Mr Sowerberry continued, "but only for children. It would be very new to have a mourner leading the procession who was in proportion, my dear."

Mrs Sowerberry was greatly taken by the novelty of this idea, but as she was much too proud to say so, she merely asked sharply why her husband had not thought of it before. Mr Sowerberry took this to be an agreement to his proposition, and it was decided that Oliver should be speedily taught an undertaker's trade.

It was a sickly season just at this time. In a commercial phrase, coffins were up; and in the course of the next few weeks Oliver acquired a great deal of experience. The success of Mr Sowerberry's ingenious idea exceeded all expectations. Many were the mournful processions which little Oliver headed, in a hatband reaching down to his knees, to the admiration and emotion of all the mothers in the town.

Perhaps it was jealousy, but throughout this time, Noah Claypole taunted Oliver whenever he could. He pulled his hair; he boxed his ears. But nothing he did could make Oliver cry. Then one morning he said, "How's your mother, Work'us Boy?"

"She's dead," replied Oliver. "And don't say anything about her!"

"What did she die of, Work'us?" said Noah.

"Of a broken heart, an old nurse told me," replied Oliver.

"It's as well she died when she did," continued Noah. "She'd be in prison or hung by now. A right bad 'un, she was."

Crimson with fury, Oliver started up, overthrew the chair and table, seized Noah by the throat, and shook him till his teeth chattered in his head. Then, collecting his whole force into one heavy blow, Oliver felled Noah to the ground.

"He'll murder me!" wailed Noah. "Help! Help! Oliver's gone mad!"

Noah's shouts were answered by a loud scream from Charlotte, and a louder one from Mrs Sowerberry. They ran into the room and pulled Oliver off Noah. Then they dragged him down to the cellar and locked the door. Noah ran to fetch Mr Bumble from the workhouse.

"Oh, Mr Bumble, sir!" said Noah when he found the beadle. "Oliver, sir – he tried to murder me, sir; and then he tried to murder Charlotte, and then Mrs Sowerberry!"

Mr Bumble and Noah hurried back to Mr Sowerberry's shop. Oliver was kicking hard at the cellar door. Mr Bumble put his mouth up to the keyhole and said in a stern voice, "Oliver!"

"Let me out!" replied Oliver from the inside.

"Do you know this here voice, Oliver?" said Mr Bumble.

"Yes," replied Oliver.

"Ain't you afraid of it, sir?" said Mr Bumble.

"No!" replied Oliver boldly.

Mr Bumble stepped back from the keyhole, drew himself up to his full height, and looked from one to another in astonishment.

"Oh, Mr Bumble, he must be mad," said Mrs Sowerberry.

"It's not madness, Mrs Sowerberry," replied Mr Bumble. "It's meat."

"What?" exclaimed Mrs Sowerberry.

"Meat, ma'am, meat," said Mr Bumble. "You've overfed him, ma'am."

Just then Mr Sowerberry arrived and Mrs Sowerberry explained what had happened. The undertaker dragged Oliver from the cellar.

"Noah called my mother names," Oliver started to explain.

"What if he did?" said Mrs Sowerberry. "She deserved it."

"It's a lie," said Oliver.

Mrs Sowerberry burst into tears and Mr Sowerberry felt obliged to beat Oliver. Then Oliver was sent to bed.

Alone in the gloomy workshop, Oliver hid his face in his hands and wept. The candle was burning low when he finally rose to his feet, gently opened the door, and looked out. It was a cold, dark night. The stars seemed far away and the trees threw ghostly shadows on the ground. Oliver closed the door again. In the fading light of the candle, he tied the few clothes he had into a handkerchief and waited for morning.

At first light Oliver unbolted the door, and slipped out into the street.

CHAPTER 2

Oliver reached the stile at the end of the path and climbed over on to the high road. It was eight o'clock. Though he was nearly five miles from the town, he ran, hiding behind hedges, till noon, fearing that he might be followed. Then he sat down to rest by the side of a milestone and began to think where he had better go and try to live.

The milestone next to him had written on it, in large letters, that it was seventy miles to London. London! Nobody, not even Mr Bumble, could ever find him there! He had often heard, too, the old men in the workhouse say that there were ways to make a living in London that those who had been bred in the country had no idea of. It was just the place for a homeless boy. With all these thoughts in his head, Oliver jumped up and walked on again.

Oliver walked twenty miles that day, and all that time had nothing but a crust of dry bread to eat and a few cupfuls of water to drink, which he begged at the cottages by the roadside. When night came, he turned into a meadow, and creeping under a haystack, fell fast asleep.

He felt cold and stiff when he got up next morning, and very hungry. He exchanged his only penny – a gift from Mr Sowerberry after some funeral in which he had acquitted himself more than ordinarily well – for a small loaf in the very first village he passed through. He had walked no more than twelve miles when night fell again. His feet were sore, and his legs so weak that they trembled beneath him.

The next morning, still weary, he set off again. In some villages, large painted boards warned that anyone who begged would be sent to jail. Oliver hurried out of those villages as quickly as he could. In others he stood around the inn-yards, hoping that a passer-by would drop him a penny. Usually, though, the landlady ordered him away, as she was sure he had come to steal something. If he begged at a farmer's house, ten to one but they threatened to set the dog on him.

Early on the seventh morning after he had left the Sowerberrys', Oliver arrived at the little town of Barnet, just north of London. The window shutters were closed, the street was empty, no one had yet woken up. Oliver sat down on the first doorstep he came to.

One by one the shutters were opened and people began to come out on to the street. A few gazed at Oliver for a moment as they passed, but no one stopped to speak.

Oliver had been sitting on the step for a while, gazing at the coaches as they passed through and thinking how strange it was that they could travel in a few hours the distance it had taken him a whole week to cover, when he noticed that a boy was staring at him from the opposite side of the street. Oliver stared back. The boy crossed the street and walked up to him.

"Hullo! What's the row?"

The boy was about Oliver's age, but one of the oddest-looking boys Oliver had ever seen. He had big ears and a flat brow, and was covered with dirt. He was short for his age, with rather bow legs, and little, sharp eyes. His hat was stuck on top of his head so lightly that it looked as if it might fall off at any moment. The boy wore a man's coat, which reached nearly to the ground. He had turned the cuffs back, halfway up his arms, to get his hands out of the sleeves.

"Hullo! What's the row?" the stranger said again.

"I'm very hungry and tired," answered Oliver. "I've been walking for seven days."

"Seven days?" said the boy. "Come on. You want food, and you shall have it. I need something to eat myself."

Pulling Oliver to his feet, the stranger took him to the chandler's nearby, where he bought ham and bread. He then led Oliver to a small public house and went through to a room at the back. The boy ordered beer, and at his new friend's bidding Oliver helped himself to the food and drink.

"Going to London?" asked the strange boy when Oliver had finished his meal.

"Yes."

"Got anywhere to stay?"

"No."

"Money?"

"No."

The strange boy whistled and put his hands in his pockets.

"Do you live in London?" asked Oliver.

"Yes, I do," replied the boy. "I suppose you want some place to sleep tonight, don't you?"

"I do, indeed," answered Oliver.

"I've got to be in London tonight, and I know a 'spectable old genelman as lives there. He'll give you lodgings for nothink."

This unexpected offer was too tempting to resist. Oliver, now feeling he had found a friend, began to talk more with the strange boy. He discovered that his name was Jack Dawkins, and that he was cared for by the elderly gentleman he had just spoken of. Dawkins also told him that he had a nickname, "The Artful Dodger".

The two set off for London, but as Dawkins objected to their arriving before nightfall, it was nearly eleven o'clock when they reached the outskirts. Then he led Oliver through a maze of streets into the centre of the city.

Oliver looked about him as they went along. He had never seen a dirtier place. The streets were narrow and muddy and the air was heavy with a filthy stench. There were a great many small shops, and there seemed to be screaming children everywhere. Off from the main streets were yards crowded with little, dingy houses.

Oliver was just wondering if he should run away, when they reached the bottom of a hill. Dawkins, catching him by the arm, pushed open the door of a house, and drawing them into the passageway, closed it behind him.

"Now then!" cried someone from below, in reply to a whistle from Dawkins.

The light of a feeble candle gleamed on the wall at the far end of the passageway, and a man's face peeped out.

"There's two on you," said the man, pushing the candle farther out, and shading his eyes with his hand. "Who's t'other one?"

"A new pal," replied Dawkins, pulling Oliver forward.

"Where did he come from?"

"Greenland. Is Fagin upstairs?"

"Yes, he's sortin' the wipes. Up with you!" The candle was drawn back, and the face disappeared.

Oliver, feeling his way with one hand, and having the other firmly grasped by his companion, climbed the dark and broken stairs. At the top Dawkins threw open the door of a back room and pulled Oliver in after him.

The walls and ceiling of the room were black with age and dirt. There was a wooden table in front of a fire, upon which were a candle stuck in a ginger-beer bottle, two or three pewter pots, a loaf and butter, and a plate. In a frying pan, which was on the fire, and which was tied to the mantel shelf by a string, some sausages were cooking. Standing over them, with a toasting fork in his hand, was a very old man, whose shrivelled face was covered by a matted red beard. He was dividing his attention between the frying pan and the clothesline, on which a great many silk handkerchiefs were hanging.

Seated at the table were four or five boys. They all crowded around Dawkins as he whispered a few words to the old man, then they turned and grinned at Oliver. So did the old man, toasting fork in hand.

"This, Fagin," said Dawkins, "is my friend Oliver Twist."

Fagin grinned, took Oliver's hand, and bowed. "We are very glad to see you, Oliver," he said. "Dodger, take off the sausages and pull up a tub near the fire for Oliver. Ah! You're staring at the pocket-handkerchiefs, eh, my dear! There are a good many of 'em, ain't there? We've just taken 'em out, ready for the wash, that's all. Ha! Ha!"

The others joined in the laughter, then they had their supper. Fagin gave Oliver some hot gin and water, telling him he must drink it quickly, because another boy wanted his glass. Oliver did as he was told. Soon afterwards he felt himself gently lifted on to some sacks, where he fell fast asleep.

It was late next morning when Oliver began to wake. There was no one else in the room but Fagin, who was boiling some coffee in a saucepan for breakfast and whistling softly to himself. When the coffee was done, Fagin turned around and looked at Oliver. He called him by his name, but Oliver was still drowsy, and did not answer. Thinking Oliver was still asleep, Fagin gently locked the door and lifted out from under the floor a small box, which he placed carefully on the table. His eyes shone as he opened the lid. Pulling over an old chair to the table, he sat down and took from the box a magnificent gold watch, sparkling with jewels.

"Aha!" said Fagin, hunching his shoulders. "Fine! Very fine!"

After muttering some more, Fagin placed the watch back in the box. At least six more were pulled out from the same box, then came rings, brooches, bracelets, and other pieces of jewellery.

Just then Fagin's bright, dark eyes fell on Oliver's face. Oliver had been staring at Fagin in silence and now quickly looked away. But it was too late. Fagin knew that he had been watched. He closed the lid of the box with a loud crash, and laying his hand on a bread knife which was on the table, jumped up in fury.

"What are you watching me for? Why are you awake? What have you seen?

Fagin grinned, took Oliver's hand, and bowed.

Speak, boy! Quick!"

"I couldn't sleep any longer, sir," replied Oliver. "I'm very sorry if I disturbed you, sir."

"You were not awake an hour ago?" asked Fagin, glaring at Oliver.

"No! No!" replied Oliver.

"Are you sure?" cried Fagin, with a fiercer look than before.

"I promise I was not, sir," replied Oliver earnestly.

"Tut, tut, my dear," said Fagin, suddenly resuming his old manner and playing with the knife a little before he laid it down, as if to pretend that he had not meant to pick it up. "Of course, I know that, my dear. I only tried to frighten you. You're a brave boy, Oliver." Fagin rubbed his hands with a chuckle, but glanced uneasily at the box nevertheless.

"Did you see any of those pretty things, my dear?" said Fagin, laying his hand on the box.

"Yes, sir," replied Oliver.

"Ah!" said Fagin, turning pale. "They – they're mine, Oliver. All I have to live on, in my old age. People call me a miser, my dear. Only a miser, that's all."

Oliver thought the old man must definitely be a miser to live in such a dirty place, with so many watches. But thinking perhaps that his fondness for the Dodger and all the other boys cost him a good deal of money, he only looked respectfully at Fagin and asked if he might get up.

"Certainly, my dear," replied the old gentleman. "There's a pitcher of water in the corner by the door. Bring it here, and I'll give you a basin to wash in."

Oliver got up, walked across the room, and picked up the pitcher. When he turned around, the box was gone.

He had just washed himself when the Dodger returned, accompanied by a young friend who was introduced to him as Charley Bates. The four sat down to breakfast.

"Well," said Fagin to the Dodger. "I hope you've been hard at work this morning."

"Very hard," replied the Dodger.

"Good boys!" said Fagin. "What have *you* got, Dodger?"

"A couple of pocketbooks," replied the Dodger.

"Lined?" inquired Fagin.

"Pretty much," replied the Dodger, producing two pocketbooks, one green and the other red.

"Not as heavy as they might be," said Fagin after looking at the insides carefully, "but very nicely made. Ingenious workman, isn't he, Oliver?"

"Very, sir," said Oliver. Charley Bates roared with laughter. Oliver was surprised. He did not see what there was to laugh at.

"And what have you got?" said Fagin to Charley Bates.

"Wipes," answered Charley, producing four pocket-handkerchiefs.

"Well," said Fagin, looking at them carefully. "They're very good ones. Very. You haven't attended well to the stitching, though, Charley, so it will have to be picked out with a needle, and we'll teach Oliver how to do it, shall we?"

"If you please, sir," said Oliver.

"You'd like to be able to make pocket-handkerchiefs as easy as Charley Bates, wouldn't you?" said Fagin.

"Very much, if you'll teach me, sir," replied Oliver.

Charley Bates roared with laughter again, but the Dodger said nothing.

When breakfast was cleared away, Fagin and the two boys played a very curious game. Fagin, placing a snuffbox in one pocket of his trousers, a wallet in the other, and a watch in his waistcoat pocket, and sticking a mock diamond pin in his shirt, buttoned his coat tight around him. Then after putting his spectacle-case and handkerchief in his pockets, he trotted up and down the room with a stick. Sometimes he stopped at the fireplace, and sometimes at the door, pretending that he was staring in shop windows. Every time he stopped, he would look around him for thieves, and would keep slapping all his pockets in turn, to see that he hadn't lost anything, in such a funny way that Oliver laughed till he cried. All this time the two boys followed him closely, getting out of his sight so quickly every time he turned around that it was impossible to follow them. At last the Dodger trod on Fagin's toes, while Charley stumbled up against him, and in that one moment they took from him, with extraordinary speed, snuffbox, wallet, watch-guard, chain, shirt-pin, pocket-handkerchief, even the spectacle-case. If Fagin felt a hand in any one of his pockets, he cried out where it was, and then the game began all over again.

When this game had been played a great many times, a couple of young ladies called to see the Dodger and Charley Bates. One was called Bet, the other Nancy. They both had long hair and looked rather untidy. They were not exactly pretty, but they had a great deal of colour in their faces. Oliver thought them very nice girls indeed.

Bet and Nancy stayed a long while. At length Charley suggested they go out, and he, the Dodger and the two girls left, Fagin having kindly given them some money to spend.

"There," said Fagin to Oliver. "They have gone out for the day."

"Have they finished work, sir?" asked Oliver.

"Yes," said Fagin. "Unless they should unexpectedly come across any. Copy them, Oliver. Do everything they ask you, and take their advice in all matters, especially the Dodger's. He'll be a great man himself, and will make you one too, if you follow him. Is my handkerchief hanging out of my pocket, my dear?" asked Fagin, stopping short.

"Yes, sir," said Oliver.

"See if you can take it out, without my feeling it, as you saw them do when we were playing this morning."

Oliver held up the flap of the pocket with one hand, as he had seen the Dodger hold it, and drew the handkerchief lightly out with the other.

"Is it gone?" cried Fagin.

"Here it is, sir," said Oliver, showing it in his hand.

"You're a clever boy," said Fagin, patting Oliver on the head approvingly. "I never saw a sharper lad. Here's a shilling for you. If you go on like this, you'll be the greatest man of the time. And now come here, and I'll show you how to take the stitching out of the handkerchiefs."

Oliver wondered what picking Fagin's pocket had to do with being a great man. But thinking that Fagin must know best, he followed him to the table and was soon unpicking the stitched initials from pocket-handkerchiefs.

CHAPTER 3

For many days Oliver worked in Fagin's room, unpicking the initials from pocket-handkerchiefs. At length he began to miss the fresh air and often asked Fagin if he could go out to work with the Dodger and Charley Bates.

Finally one morning Oliver obtained the permission he had wanted for so long. There had been no handkerchiefs to work on for several days and Fagin told Oliver he might go, looked after by the Dodger and Charley.

The three boys went out, the Dodger with his coat-sleeves rolled up and his hat cocked as usual. Charley Bates walked along with his hands in his pockets. Oliver, walking between them, wondered where they were going, and what they were going to do.

They were just coming out of a narrow passageway, when the Dodger suddenly stopped, and laying his finger on his lip, pulled his friends back again.

"What's the matter?" demanded Oliver.

"Ssshh," replied the Dodger. "Do you see that old man at the bookstall?"

"The gentleman over there?" said Oliver. "Yes, I see him."

"He'll do," said the Dodger.

"Perfect," remarked Charley Bates.

Oliver looked from one to the other in surprise, but he was not allowed to ask any questions, for the two boys walked stealthily across the road and crept up close behind the old gentleman. Oliver walked a few paces behind them, and not knowing whether to go on or go back, stood watching in amazement.

The old gentleman was a very respectable-looking character, with a powdered head and gold spectacles. He was dressed in a bottle-green coat with a black velvet collar, wore white trousers, and carried a smart bamboo cane under his arm. He had picked up a book from the stall, and stood reading away. He did not seem aware of the bookstall, or the street, and did not see the boys.

To Oliver's horror he saw the Dodger plunge his hand into the old gentleman's pocket and draw out a handkerchief, which he gave to Charley Bates. The two then ran away as fast as their legs would carry them.

In a second the whole mystery of the handkerchiefs, and the watches, and the jewels, and Fagin hit Oliver. He stood for a moment with the blood tingling through his veins from terror. Then, confused and frightened, he took to his heels and ran off as fast as he could.

Just as he started to run, the old gentleman, putting his hand in his pocket and realizing his handkerchief was gone, turned around. Seeing Oliver running away so fast, he assumed him to be the thief. Shouting, "Stop, thief!" with all his might, he made off after him, book in hand.

But the old gentleman was not the only one to start shouting. The Dodger and Charley Bates, hiding in a doorway around the corner, heard the cry and saw Oliver running. Guessing what had happened, they ran out, and shouting, "Stop thief!" too, joined the chase.

People in the streets heard the cries. The wagon driver left his wagon; the butcher put down his tray; the baker put down his basket; the milkman put down his bucket; the errand boy, his parcels; the schoolboy, his marbles. They all started to run helter-skelter, tearing, yelling, screaming, knocking down passers-by as they turned corners.

"Stop thief! Stop thief!" The cry was taken up by a hundred voices, and the crowd grew at every turning. Away they flew, splashing through the mud.

"Stop thief! Stop thief!"

Stopped at last! Oliver fell on the pavement and the crowd gathered around him, jostling and struggling to catch a glimpse.

Oliver lay covered with mud and dust, looking at the heap of faces that surrounded him, when the old gentleman was pushed into the circle.

"Is this the boy, sir?" someone asked.

"Yes," said the gentleman, "I'm afraid it is the boy. Poor fellow. He has hurt himself."

Just then a police officer made his way through the crowd and seized Oliver by the collar.

"Come on, get up," said the policeman roughly.

"It wasn't me, sir. It was two other boys," said Oliver, looking around. "They are here somewhere."

"Oh no, they're not," said the policeman. Which was true, for the Dodger and Charley Bates had slipped off down the first alleyway they came to. "Come on, get up!"

Oliver stood up and was at once pulled along the streets by his jacket collar. The old gentleman walked with them by the policeman's side. From their hiding place the Dodger and Charley Bates shouted in triumph, and ran off.

Oliver was taken to the police station. A fat man with a bunch of keys came up to him. "What's the matter now?" he asked.

"A young pickpocket," said the policeman.

"Are you the one who's been robbed?" asked the man with the keys, turning to Mr Brownlow.

"Yes, I am," replied the old gentleman, "but I'm not sure that this boy actually took the handkerchief. I would rather not press the case."

"Must go before the judge now, sir," replied the man.

Oliver was led to a stone cell and locked up.

The old gentleman looked sorrowful as Oliver was taken away. "There's something in that boy's face," he said to himself, tapping his chin thoughtfully. "He looked like. . . No, it must be my imagination. . ." And he sat down and began to read his book.

He was roused by a touch on the shoulder and a request from the man with the keys to follow him into the office. He closed his book and was ushered in before the judge, Mr Fang.

Mr Fang sat behind a bar at the far end, and on one side was a wooden pen in which Oliver had already been locked. Mr Fang was thin and stiff-necked. He had very little hair, and what he had, grew on the back and sides of his head. The old gentleman bowed respectfully.

"Who are you?" said Mr Fang.

"My name, sir, is Brownlow."

"Officer!" said Mr Fang. "What's this fellow charged with?"

"He's not charged at all, your honour," replied the officer. "He appears against the boy, your honour."

"Swear him in," said Mr Fang contemptuously. "Now, what's the charge against this boy?"

"I was standing at a bookstall. . ." Mr Brownlow began.

"Hold your tongue, sir," interrupted Mr Fang. "Policeman! Now, policeman, what is this?"

The policeman, head bowed, related how he had discovered Oliver, how he had searched him and found nothing, and how that was all he knew about it.

"Are there any witnesses?" asked Mr Fang.

"None, your honour," replied the policeman.

Mr Fang sat silent for some while, and then turning to Mr Brownlow, asked him to state his complaint against Oliver.

With many interruptions Mr Brownlow stated his case, pointing out that in the heat of the moment he had run after Oliver because he saw him running away. He hoped that the judge would believe, as he did, that the boy was not actually the thief, although he was connected with the thieves, and that he would therefore deal leniently with him.

"He has been hurt already," Mr Brownlow added. "And I fear that he is ill."

"Oh, I daresay!" sneered Mr Fang. "Come, you young vagabond. What's your name?"

Oliver tried to reply, but he was tongue-tied.

"What's his name?"

This was said to a clerk. He bent over Oliver and repeated the question, but finding him really incapable of answering, hazarded a guess.

"He says his name's Tom White, your honour," said the clerk.

"Where does he live?" asked Mr Fang.

"Where he can," replied the clerk, again pretending to receive Oliver's answer.

"Has he any parents?" Mr Fang went on.

"He says they died in his infancy, your honour," replied the clerk, guessing again.

At this point Oliver raised his head and quietly asked for a cup of water.

"Nonsense!" said Mr Fang.

"I think he really is ill, your honour," said the clerk.

"I know better," said Mr Fang.

At that moment Oliver fainted.

"I knew he was pretending," said Fang. "Let him lie there. He'll soon be tired of it. He is committed for three months' hard labour. Clear the office."

Just as a couple of policemen were preparing to carry Oliver from the room, an elderly, poor-looking man rushed in.

"Stop, stop! Don't take him away!" cried the newcomer.

"What's this? Who is this? Out! Clear the office!" cried Mr Fang.

"I *will* speak," cried the man. "I saw it all. I keep the bookstall. Mr Fang, you must hear me."

Mr Fang growled. "What have you got to say?"

"I saw three boys, two others and the prisoner here, loitering on the opposite side of the street when this gentleman was reading. The robbery was committed by another boy. I saw it done."

"The prosecutor was reading, was he?" asked Fang.

"Yes, the very book he has in his hand."

"That book?" asked Mr Fang. "Is it paid for?"

"No, it is not," said the man with a smile.

"Dear me, I forgot all about it!" exclaimed Mr Brownlow innocently.

"A nice person to charge a poor boy," said Fang. "You should think yourself fortunate that the owner of the book declines to prosecute. The boy is discharged. Clear the office!"

Mr Brownlow was shown out, with the book in one hand and the bamboo cane in the other. Oliver was discharged, and thrown out on the pavement.

"Call a coach, somebody. Quickly!" said Mr Brownlow.

A coach arrived and Oliver was carefully laid on one seat. Mr Brownlow got in and sat on the other.

"May I accompany you?" said the bookstall keeper.

"Of course!" said Mr Brownlow quickly. "Dear, dear! I have your book still! Jump in!"

The bookstall keeper got into the coach, and away they drove.

The coach rattled on until it reached a neat house in a quiet, shady street. Here, Oliver was lifted down from the coach and put to bed.

* * *

It was several days before Oliver awoke from what seemed to him to have been a long and troubled dream. He looked around him. "What room is this?" he cried. "Where have I been brought to? This is not the place I went to sleep in!"

The curtain at the bed was drawn back, and a motherly old lady got up from an armchair close by, in which she had been sewing.

"Hush, my dear," said the old lady softly. "You must be very quiet, or you will be ill again, and you have been very bad. Lie down now, there's a dear!"

With these words, the old lady very gently placed Oliver's head upon the pillow, and smoothing back his hair from his forehead, looked kindly into his face.

Oliver kept very still, partly because he was anxious to do as the old lady asked, and partly because he was still exhausted. He soon fell into a gentle doze. Later he was awakened by the light of a candle that, being brought near the bed, showed him a gentleman with a very large and loud-ticking gold watch in his hand, who felt his pulse and said that he was a great deal better.

"You *are* a great deal better, aren't you, my dear?" said the gentleman.

"Yes, thank you, sir," replied Oliver.

"Yes, I know you are," said the gentleman. "You're hungry too, aren't you?"

"No, sir," answered Oliver.

"Humph!" said the gentleman. "No, I know you're not. He is not hungry, Mrs Bedwin," said the gentleman wisely.

The old lady nodded her head, as if she thought the doctor a very clever man.

"You feel sleepy, don't you, my dear?" asked the doctor.

"No, sir," replied Oliver.

"No," said the doctor with a wise look. "You're not sleepy, nor thirsty, are you?"

"Yes, sir, rather thirsty," answered Oliver.

"Just as I expected, Mrs Bedwin," said the doctor. "It's very natural that he should be thirsty. You may give him a little tea, and some dry toast without any butter. Don't keep him too warm, but be careful you don't let him be too cold."

Mrs Bedwin curtsied and the doctor hurried away, his boots creaking in a very important way as he went downstairs.

Oliver dozed off again, and when he awoke it was nearly twelve o'clock. The old lady tenderly said goodnight soon afterwards and left him in the care of a matronly old woman who had just arrived, bringing a large nightcap with her. Putting the cap on her head and telling Oliver that she had come to sit with him, she drew her chair close to the fire and fell asleep. Every so often she would snore loudly, start up, rub her nose, then fall fast asleep again.

Oliver lay awake for some time, tracing the intricate pattern of the paper on the wall. Gradually he fell into a deep and tranquil sleep.

*   *   *

After three days Oliver was well enough to sit in an armchair, and Mrs Bedwin had him carried down to the little housekeeper's room, which belonged to her.

"It's high time you had some broth," said Mrs Bedwin, "for the doctor

35

says Mr Brownlow may come in to see you this morning, and we must look our best." And with this, Mrs Bedwin warmed up, in a saucepan, a basin full of broth.

"Do you like pictures, dear?" asked the old lady, seeing that Oliver was looking intently at a portrait which hung against the wall just opposite his chair.

"I don't know, ma'am," said Oliver. "I haven't seen many. What a beautiful face that lady has! Who is it?"

"Why, really, my dear, I don't know," answered Mrs Bedwin good-humouredly. "It's not a likeness of anybody that you or I know, I expect. It seems to strike your fancy, my dear."

"It is so very pretty," replied Oliver.

"You are sure you are not afraid of it?" said Mrs Bedwin, noticing with surprise the look of awe on Oliver's face.

"Oh, no," replied Oliver quickly, "but the eyes look so sad, and from where I sit they seem to be staring at me. It is as if the lady were alive and wanted to speak to me, but can't."

"Goodness me!" exclaimed Mrs Bedwin. "You mustn't say such things! You are weak after your illness. Let me turn your chair round to the other side, and then you won't see it. There!" she said as she moved Oliver's chair around. "You cannot see the portrait now, at all events."

Oliver *did* see the picture in his imagination, as clearly as if he had not been turned around, but decided to say no more about it. Mrs Bedwin brought him his broth, and he had scarcely swallowed the last spoonful when there was a soft knock at the door.

"Come in," said Mrs Bedwin, and in walked Mr Brownlow. He raised his spectacles on his forehead, and thrust his hands behind the skirts of his dressing-gown to take a good long look at Oliver.

"How do you feel, my dear?" he asked.

"Very happy, sir," replied Oliver. "And very grateful, sir, for your goodness to me."

"Good boy," said Mr Brownlow. "Have you given him any nourishment,

Bedwin?"

"He has just had a basin of strong broth, sir," replied Mrs Bedwin.

"Ugh!" said Mr Brownlow with a shudder. "A couple of glasses of port wine would have done him a great deal more good, wouldn't they, Tom White, eh?"

"My name is Oliver, sir," the boy answered with a look of great astonishment.

"Oliver," said Mr Brownlow. "Oliver what?"

"Twist, sir. Oliver Twist."

"Queer name!" said Mr Brownlow. "What made you tell the judge your name was White?"

"I never told him so, sir," replied Oliver in amazement.

This sounded so like a lie that Mr Brownlow looked sternly into Oliver's face. It was impossible to doubt him. He looked as if he was telling the truth.

"Some mistake," said Mr Brownlow. Then, as he stared again at Oliver's face, the old idea of resemblance between his features and some familiar face came upon him so strongly that he could not withdraw his gaze.

"I hope you are not angry with me, sir?" said Oliver, looking up at Mr Brownlow.

"No, no!" replied Mr Brownlow. "Goodness! What's this? Bedwin, look there!" he suddenly exclaimed.

As he spoke he pointed to the picture on the wall above Oliver's head, and then to Oliver's face. The eyes, the head, the mouth: every feature was the same.

Oliver had no idea what was the cause of this sudden exclamation. Unable to see the picture behind him, he could not guess what Mr Brownlow was talking about.

"What's this? Bedwin, look there!" Mr Brownlow suddenly exclaimed.

CHAPTER 4

When the Dodger and Charley Bates had joined the crowd that chased Oliver, they had done so to save themselves from being caught. Now that the chase was over, they were safe.

"What'll Fagin say?" asked the Dodger.

"What?" repeated Charley Bates.

"Ah, what?" said the Dodger.

"Why, what should he say?" inquired Charley, stopping suddenly, for the Dodger was serious.

The Dodger did not reply. Putting his hat on again, he slunk down the alleyway. Charley Bates followed with a thoughtful expression.

The noise of footsteps on the stairs aroused Fagin as he sat over the fire with a sausage and a small loaf. There was a rascally look on his face as he turned around and listened.

"How's this?" he muttered. "Only two of 'em? Where's the third?"

The footsteps approached nearer. They reached the landing. The door was slowly opened, and the Dodger and Charley Bates entered, closing it behind them.

"Where's Oliver?" asked Fagin, rising with a menacing look. "Where's the boy?"

The Dodger and Charley Bates looked uneasily at each other, but said nothing.

"What's become of the boy?" asked Fagin, seizing the Dodger tightly by the collar. "Speak out, or I'll throttle you!"

"The police have got him," said the Dodger sullenly. "Let go o' me, will you!" And swinging himself out of Fagin's grasp, the Dodger snatched up the toasting fork and made a pass at Fagin's waistcoat. Fagin jumped back, and seizing up a pot, prepared to hurl it at the Dodger's head. But just at that moment Charley Bates let out a great howl, and Fagin suddenly changed direction and flung it full at the young gentleman.

"What!" growled a deep voice. "Who pitched that 'ere at me? What's it all about, Fagin?"

The man who growled these words was a stoutly built fellow of about thirty-five, in a black velveteen coat, very dirty trousers, lace-up half boots and grey cotton stockings that enclosed a thick pair of legs with large calves. He had a brown hat on his head and a dirty handkerchief around his neck. He had a broad, heavy face and two scowling eyes.

"Come in, d'you hear?" growled the man again.

A mangy white dog skulked into the room.

"Why didn't you come in afore? Lie down!"

The dog coiled himself up in a corner very quietly, without uttering a sound.

"What are you up to? Ill-treating the boys. . ."

"Hush, Mr Sikes," said Fagin, trembling. "Not so loud."

"None of your mistering," replied the ruffian. "You always mean trouble when you come to that. You know my name."

"Well then – Bill Sikes," said Fagin apologetically. "You seem out of humour, Bill."

"Perhaps I am," replied Sikes. "I should think *you* was rather out of sorts too, unless you mean as little harm when you throw pots about you as you do when you blab and – "

"Are you mad?" said Fagin, pointing towards the boys.

Sikes said no more and looked at the two boys. Dodger described Oliver's capture, with such alterations or improvements on the truth as seemed to him most advisable under the circumstances.

"I'm afraid," said Fagin, "that he may say something which will get us into trouble."

"That's very likely," returned Sikes with a malicious grin. "You're blowed upon, Fagin."

"And I'm afraid, you see," continued Fagin, "that if the game was up with us, it might be up with a good many more, and it would come out worse for you than it would for me. . ."

There was a long pause. Then Sikes said, "Somebody must find out wot's been done at the office. If he hasn't told tales, and is in jail, then there's no fear till he comes out again. And then he must be taken care of. You must get hold of him somehow."

Fagin nodded. The difficulty was that not one of them in the room wanted to go near the police station.

Just then Bet and Nancy arrived. "The very thing!" said Fagin. "Bet will go, won't you, my dear?"

"Where?" asked Bet.

"Only just up to the office," said Fagin coaxingly. But Bet refused.

Fagin turned to Nancy. "My dear," he said, "what do you say?"

"No, Fagin," replied Nancy.

"What do you mean by that?" said Sikes. "She'll go, Fagin."

"No, she won't, Fagin," said Nancy.

"Yes, she will, Fagin," said Sikes.

Sikes was right. With a clean white apron tied over her gown and wearing a straw bonnet, both articles being provided from Fagin's stock, Nancy prepared to leave.

"Wait a moment," said Fagin, producing a little covered basket. "Carry that in one hand. It looks much more respectable, my dear."

"Give her a door key to carry in her other one," said Sikes. "It looks real and genuine like."

"Oh, my brother! My poor, dear, sweet little brother!" exclaimed Nancy, bursting into tears. "What has become of him! Where have they taken him?"

Having uttered these words in a most heartbroken tone, Nancy paused, winked to the company, and disappeared.

She made her way to the police station. Entering by the back gate, she tapped softly with the key at one of the cell doors, and listened. There was no sound. "Nolly?" she whispered. "Oliver?"

There was nobody in the cell but a tramp.

"Is there a little boy here?" asked Nancy.

"No," replied the tramp.

Nancy went to find the clerk, and crying bitterly, demanded that her brother be set free.

"I haven't got him, my dear," said the man.

"Where is he?" screamed Nancy.

"Why, the gentleman's got him," replied the clerk.

"What gentleman?" exclaimed Nancy.

The clerk told Nancy that Oliver had been taken ill in the office, and discharged when a witness proved the robbery had been committed by another boy. The old gentleman had taken him to his own residence.

In a state of doubt and uncertainty, Nancy ran all the way back to Fagin's house.

As soon as Sikes heard her story, he called to his dog and left.

"We must find him," said Fagin. "Out, all of you! Don't stop here a minute." With these words, he pushed them from the room and locked and barred the door. Then he drew out the box that Oliver had seen, opened it, and quickly hid the watches and jewellery in his pockets.

"He has not betrayed us yet," said Fagin as he filled his pockets. "If he means to talk to his new friends, we may stop him yet."

* * *

Oliver sat in Mrs Bedwin's room, looking around for the picture.

"Ah!" said the housekeeper, watching the direction of Oliver's eyes. "It's gone, you see."

"Why have they taken it away?"

"Mr Brownlow said that as it seemed to worry you, perhaps it might prevent your getting well," answered Mrs Bedwin.

"Oh, no. It didn't worry me. I liked to see it," exclaimed Oliver.

But there was no more mention of the picture. Oliver spent happy days with Mrs Bedwin, and as soon as he was well enough, Mr Brownlow provided him with a new suit, cap, and pair of shoes.

One evening a message came from Mr Brownlow, asking to see Oliver in his study. Oliver went and tapped at the study door. On Mr Brownlow calling to him to come in, he found himself in a little back room full of books, with a window looking into some pretty gardens. There was a table drawn up before the window, at which Mr Brownlow was seated. When he saw Oliver, he told him to come and sit down. Oliver obeyed.

"Now," said Mr Brownlow in a serious manner, "I want you to pay attention, my boy, to what I am going to say."

"Oh, don't tell me you are going to send me away, sir!" exclaimed Oliver.

"My dear child," said the old gentleman, "you need not be afraid of my deserting you, unless you give me cause. Let me hear your story, where you come from, who brought you up, and how you got into the company in which I found you. Speak the truth, and you shall not be friendless while I live."

Oliver was at the point of beginning his story, when there was a knock at the door, and a servant announced Mr Grimwig had arrived.

"Shall I go downstairs, sir?" asked Oliver.

"No," replied Mr Brownlow. "I would rather you remained here."

At this moment a stout and rather lame old gentleman walked into the room. He was dressed in a blue coat, striped waistcoat, breeches and gaiters, and a broad-brimmed white hat. A shirt frill stuck out from his waistcoat, and a very long steel watch-chain, with nothing but a key at the end, dangled below it. He had a manner of screwing his head on one side when he spoke, and of looking out of the corners of his eyes at the same time.

"Hallo! What's that?" said Mr Grimwig, looking at Oliver.

"This is young Oliver Twist, whom we were speaking about," said Mr Brownlow.

"How are you, boy?" asked Mr Grimwig gruffly.

"A great deal better, thank you, sir," replied Oliver.

Mr Brownlow, seeming to anticipate that Mr Grimwig was about to say something disagreeable, asked Oliver to go downstairs and tell Mrs Bedwin they were ready for tea. Oliver was happy to go. He did not like Mr Grimwig's manner.

At tea Mr Grimwig asked Mr Brownlow, "And when are you going to hear a full and true account of the life and adventures of Oliver Twist?"

"Tomorrow morning," replied Mr Brownlow. "I would rather he was alone with me at the time." Mr Brownlow smiled at Oliver and said, "Come up to me tomorrow morning at ten o'clock, my dear."

"Yes, sir," replied Oliver. He answered with some hesitation, confused by Mr Grimwig's looking so hard at him.

"I'll tell you what," whispered Mr Grimwig to Mr Brownlow, "he won't come up to you tomorrow morning. I saw him hesitate. He is deceiving you, my good friend."

"I'll swear he is not," replied Mr Brownlow.

Just then Mrs Bedwin brought in a small parcel of books, which Mr Brownlow had that morning purchased at the bookstall.

"Stop the boy who delivered these, Mrs Bedwin!" said Mr Brownlow. "There are some books to go back."

The street door was opened, but there was no boy in sight.

"Dear me," exclaimed Mr Brownlow. "I particularly wished those books to be returned tonight."

"Send Oliver with them," said Mr Grimwig with an ironical smile. "He will be sure to deliver them safely, you know."

"Yes, do let me take them, sir," said Oliver.

"You shall go," said Mr Brownlow. "The books are on a chair by my table. Fetch them down. You are to say that you have brought the books back, and that you have come to pay the four pound ten I owe him. This is a five-pound note, so you will have to bring me back ten shillings change."

"I won't be ten minutes, sir," replied Oliver. Having buttoned up the bank note in his jacket pocket, he bowed and left the room.

"Let me see. He'll be back in twenty minutes at the longest," said Mr Brownlow, pulling out his watch and placing it on the table.

"You really expect him to come back, do you?" inquired Mr Grimwig.

"Don't you?" smiled Mr Brownlow.

"No," said Mr Grimwig. "I do not. The boy has a new suit of clothes, a set of valuable books, and a five-pound note in his pocket.  He'll join his old friends the thieves. If ever that boy returns, I'll eat my head!"

With these words he drew his chair closer to the table and there the two friends sat, with the watch between them.

* * *

Oliver made his way to the bookstall. He was walking along, thinking how happy and contented he felt, when he was startled by a young woman screaming out very loudly, "Oh, my dear brother!" And he had hardly looked up to see what the matter was, when he was stopped by having a pair of arms thrown tight around his neck.

"Don't," cried Oliver, struggling. "Let go of me. Who is it?"

"Come home directly, you cruel boy!" said the young woman.

"What's the matter, ma'am?" inquired a woman who had come out when she heard the screams.

"He ran away," replied the young woman. "Near a month ago, from his parents, and went and joined a set of thieves and bad characters."

"Young wretch!" said the woman.

"I am not! Why, it's Nancy!" said Oliver as he saw the young woman's face for the first time.

"You see, he knows me!" cried Nancy.

"What's going on?" said a man, suddenly appearing with a white dog at his heels. "Young Oliver! Come home directly."

"I don't belong to them. I don't know them. Help! Help!" cried Oliver, struggling in the man's powerful grasp.

"Yes, I'll help you, you young rascal!" said the man. "What books are these? You've been stealing again, haven't you?" With these words the man tore the books from Oliver's grasp and struck him on the head.

In another moment Oliver was dragged into a labyrinth of dark, narrow courts.

*   *   *

The gas lamps were lit. Mrs Bedwin was waiting anxiously at the open door; and still the two old gentlemen sat in the dark parlour, with the watch between them.

A few days later in a public house in London, a fat beadle took his glass and drew his chair nearer to the fire. Then he began to read his paper. The first paragraph that Mr Bumble saw was an advertisement:

Oliver was dragged into a labyrinth of dark, narrow courts.

FIVE GUINEAS REWARD

A young boy, named Oliver Twist, absconded, or was enticed, on Thursday evening last, from his home and has not since been heard of. The above reward will be paid to any person who will give such information as will lead to the discovery of the said Oliver Twist, or will throw any light upon his history.

There then followed a full description of Oliver, with the name and address of Mr Brownlow at the bottom.

Mr Bumble read the advertisement slowly several times, and then within five minutes was on his way to Mr Brownlow's residence.

"Is Mr Brownlow at home?" inquired Mr Bumble of the girl who opened the door. He explained why he had come, and Mrs Bedwin, who had been listening at the parlour door, hurried into the hallway.

"Come in, come in," said the old lady.

Mr Bumble was shown into the back study, where Mr Brownlow sat with Mr Grimwig.

"Now, sir, you come because you saw the advertisement?"

"Yes, sir," said Mr Bumble.

"What do you know of the boy?" asked Mr Brownlow.

"You don't know any good of him, do you?" asked Mr Grimwig.

Mr Bumble shook his head solemnly.

"You see?" said Mr Grimwig triumphantly.

Mr Brownlow asked Mr Bumble to tell what he knew of Oliver, in as few words as possible. Mr Bumble did as he was asked. Oliver was an orphan. From his birth he had displayed no better qualities than treachery and ingratitude. He had made a cowardly attack on an innocent boy and then run away from his master's house. As proof, Mr Bumble laid upon the table the papers bearing his credentials.

"I fear it is all too true," said Mr Brownlow sorrowfully, after looking at the papers. He gave Mr Bumble the five guineas, and the beadle left.

Mr Brownlow paced the room for some minutes. At length he stopped and rang the bell violently.

"Mrs Bedwin," said Mr Brownlow when the housekeeper appeared, "that boy Oliver is an imposter."

"It can't be, sir," said the old lady passionately.

"I tell you he is," replied the old gentleman. "Never let me hear the boy's name again. Never. Never, on any pretence."

There were sad hearts at Mr Brownlow's that night.

CHAPTER 5

The narrow streets and courts at length ended in a large open space. Sikes slackened his pace, and turning to Oliver, roughly ordered him to take hold of Nancy's hand.

"Do you hear?" growled Sikes as Oliver hesitated. He held out his hand, which Nancy clasped tightly in hers.

"Here, Bull's-eye!" said Sikes.

The dog looked up and growled.

"See here, Bull's-eye!" said Sikes, putting his hand to Oliver's throat. "If he speaks ever so soft a word, hold him!"

The dog growled again, and licking his lips, eyed Oliver.

They walked on for a full half-hour. At last they turned into a filthy, narrow street. Bull's-eye ran forward and stopped before the door of a shop that was closed.

"All right," cried Sikes, glancing cautiously about.

Nancy stooped below the shutters and Oliver heard the sound of a bell. They crossed to the opposite side of the street, and stood for a few moments under a lamp. A sash-window was gently raised, and soon afterwards the door softly opened. Sikes seized Oliver by the collar and all three went quickly inside.

The passage was completely dark.

"Anybody here?" inquired Sikes.

"No," replied a voice, which Oliver thought he had heard before.

"Is the old 'un here?" asked Sikes.

"Yes," replied the voice.

"Give us a light," said Sikes, "or we shall go breaking our legs, or treading on the dog."

"Stand still a moment and I'll get you one," replied the voice. In another minute the Artful Dodger appeared at the top of the stairs. He carried in his right hand a candle stuck on the end of a stick.

The Dodger grinned at Oliver and beckoned the three to follow him. They climbed the stairs and crossed the empty kitchen of the new hideout, and opening the door of a low, earthy-smelling room, were greeted with a shout of laughter.

"Oh!" cried Charley Bates. "Oh, look at his clothes, Fagin! Super-fine cloth! Nothing but a gentleman, Fagin!"

"Delighted to see you looking so well, my dear," said Fagin, bowing with mock humility. "The Dodger shall give you another suit, my dear, for fear you should spoil that Sunday one. Why didn't you write, my dear, and say you were coming? We'd have got something warm for supper."

At that instant the Dodger drew out the five-pound note from Oliver's pocket.

"Hallo! What's that?" asked Sikes, stepping forward as Fagin grabbed the note. "That's mine, Fagin."

"No, no," said Fagin. "Mine, Bill, mine."

"If that isn't mine!" said Sikes, putting on his hat, "mine and Nancy's that is, I'll take the boy back again."

"This is hardly fair, Bill, hardly fair," said Fagin.

"Fair or not fair," replied Sikes, "hand over, I tell you. Do you think Nancy and me has got nothing else to do with our time but to spend it scouting after, and kidnapping every

51

young boy as gets grabbed through you? Give it here, you avaricious old skeleton. Give it here!"

With this, Sikes plucked the note from Fagin's fingers, folded it up, and tied it in his neckerchief.

Oliver looked at Sikes, then at Fagin. Suddenly he jumped to his feet and tore wildly from the room, uttering shrieks for help.

"Keep back the dog, Bill," cried Nancy, jumping to the door and closing it after Fagin, the Dodger and Charley Bates darted out in pursuit. "Keep back the dog. He'll tear the boy to pieces."

"Serve him right!" cried Sikes. "Stand off from me, or I'll split your head against the wall!"

"I don't care for that, Bill," screamed Nancy, struggling with Sikes. "The child shan't be torn down by the dog unless you kill me first."

"Shan't he!" said Sikes, setting his teeth. "I'll soon do that if you don't keep off."

Sikes flung Nancy to the end of the room, just as Fagin and the two boys returned, dragging Oliver with them.

"So you wanted to get away, my dear, did you?" said Fagin, taking up a jagged club which lay in the corner of the fireplace. "We'll cure you of that, my young master."

Fagin hit Oliver sharply on the shoulders with the club, and was raising it for a second time when Nancy, rushing forward, snatched it from his hand and flung it into the fire.

"I won't stand by and see it done, Fagin," cried the girl. "You've got the boy, and what more would you have?"

"Keep quiet!" interrupted Sikes, with a growl he was more accustomed to using when addressing his dog, "or I'll quiet you for a good long time to come. You're a nice one to take up the humane and genteel side! A pretty subject for a child, as you call him, to make a friend of!"

"I wish I had been struck dead in the street before I had lent a hand in bringing him here. He's a thief, a liar, a devil, all that's bad, from this night forth. Isn't that enough, without blows?"

"Come, come, Sikes," said Fagin, "we must have civil words. Civil words, Bill."

"Civil words!" cried Nancy. "Civil words, you villain!"

"I shall do you a mischief," cried Fagin, "if you say much more!"

Nancy said nothing more. Instead she rushed for Fagin, but Sikes seized her wrists, upon which she made a few ineffectual struggles, and fainted.

"She's all right now," said Sikes, laying her down in a corner.

Fagin wiped his forehead and smiled. "Charley, show Oliver to bed," he said.

"I suppose he'd better not wear his best clothes tomorrow, Fagin, had he?" inquired Charley.

"Certainly not," replied Fagin, grinning.

Charley led Oliver into the kitchen, where there were two beds, and produced an old suit of clothes.

"Pull off the smart ones," said Charley, "and I'll give them to Fagin to take care of."

Oliver obeyed. Charley departed, leaving Oliver in the dark, and locking the door behind him. Sick and weary, Oliver fell sound asleep.

The next day, when the Dodger and Charley Bates had gone out, Fagin read Oliver a long lecture on the sin of ingratitude, of which he clearly showed he had been guilty. He told Oliver of another young boy who had run to the police with stories about his friends, but he had been hanged before he had managed to tell them.

Oliver's blood ran cold as he listened to Fagin's words, and half-understood the dark threats conveyed in them.

Fagin, patting Oliver on the head, said that if he kept quiet, he was sure they could be friends yet. Then, taking his hat and covering himself with an old patched great-coat, he went out and locked the door behind him.

It was cold and windy outside. Fagin buttoned his coat tight around him and pulled the collar up over his ears. He paused as the door was locked and chained behind him, and then slunk down the street as quickly as he could. He hurried along several alleys and streets and at length turned into one, lit only by a single lamp at the far end. At the door of a house he knocked. A dog growled, and a man's voice demanded who was there.

"Only me, Bill," said Fagin.

"Come in, then," said Sikes. "Lie down, you stupid dog! Don't you know Fagin when he's got a great-coat on?"

Fagin took off his coat and Bull's-eye went back to the corner, wagging his tail as he went.

"Well, my dear," said Fagin. "Ah! Nancy."

Fagin sounded a little embarrassed, for he was unsure how Nancy would receive him: they had not met since she had interfered on behalf of Oliver. All doubts were removed when Nancy took her feet off the hearth, pushed back her chair, and invited Fagin to draw up his, without saying more about it.

"Now, my dear," Fagin said to Sikes as he settled himself by the fire, "about the robbery. When is it to be done, Bill, eh? When is it to be done?"

"Not at all," replied Sikes coldly, "unless I can get a boy. I want a boy, and he mustn't be a big 'un."

Fagin nodded his head towards Nancy and indicated that he would like her to leave the room.

"Why, you don't mind Nancy, do you, Fagin?" Sikes asked. "You've known her long enough to trust her. She's not one to blab, are you, Nancy?"

"I should think not," replied Nancy, drawing her chair up to the table. "Now, Fagin, tell Bill at once about Oliver!"

"Ha! You're the sharpest girl I ever saw," said Fagin. "It *was* about Oliver I was going to speak."

"What about him?" demanded Sikes.

"He's the boy for you, my dear," whispered Fagin, grinning.

"He!" exclaimed Sikes.

"It's time he began to work," said Fagin. "Besides, the others are all too big."

"Well, he is just the size I need," said Sikes, ruminating.

"And he'll do everything you want, Bill," said Fagin. "That is, if you frighten him enough."

"Now, my dear," Fagin said, "about the robbery. When is it to be done?"

"When is it to be done?" asked Nancy.

"The night after tomorrow," replied Sikes.

"Good," said Fagin, "there's no moon."

After some discussion it was decided that Nancy should go to Fagin's the next evening and bring Oliver away with her.

When Oliver awoke the next morning, he was surprised to find that a new pair of shoes had been placed at his bedside. At first he was pleased, hoping that it might mean he was to be released; but such thoughts were quickly dispelled on his sitting down to breakfast with Fagin, who told him that he was to be taken to Bill Sikes that night.

"To. . . to. . . stay there, sir?" asked Oliver anxiously.

"No, no, my dear. Not to stay," replied Fagin. "We shouldn't like to lose you. Don't be afraid, Oliver, you shall come back to us again."

Oliver still felt very anxious, but he asked no more questions. Fagin was surly and silent till night, when he prepared to go out.

"You may burn a candle," said Fagin, putting one on the table. "And here's a book for you to read till they come to fetch you. Good night!"

"Good night," replied Oliver softly.

Fagin walked to the door, looking over his shoulder at the boy as he went. Suddenly stopping, he called him by his name.

Oliver looked up.

"Take heed, Oliver! Take heed!" said Fagin, shaking his right hand before him in a warning manner. "He's a rough man. Whatever happens, say nothing, and do what he tells you." Then Fagin gave Oliver one last ghastly grin, and nodding his head, left the room.

Oliver sat with his head in his hands. Suddenly a rustling noise aroused him.

"What's that!" he cried, catching sight of a figure standing by the door. "Who's there?"

"Me. Only me," replied a trembling voice.

Oliver raised the candle above his head and looked towards the door. It was Nancy.

"Am I going to go with you?" asked Oliver.

"Yes, I have come from Bill," replied Nancy. "You are to go with me."

"What for?" asked Oliver, recoiling.

"What for?" echoed Nancy, raising her eyes and looking away again the moment they met Oliver's face. "Oh! For no harm."

"I don't believe it," said Oliver, who had watched her closely.

Nancy turned to him. "Remember this! And don't let me suffer more for you. If I could help you, I would; but I have not the power. They don't mean to harm you. Whatever you do is no fault of yours. Hush! Give me your hand. Hurry! Your hand!"

She caught the hand which Oliver instinctively placed in hers, and blowing out the light, drew him outside. A cart was waiting and Nancy pulled Oliver in with her. The driver needed no instructions, and lashed his horse into full speed without delay. All was so hurried that Oliver had scarcely time to recollect where he was when the cart stopped at the house to which Fagin had come on the previous evening.

"This way," said Nancy, releasing Oliver's hand for the first time. "Bill!"

"Hallo!" replied Sikes, appearing at the top of the stairs. "Come on!"

Sikes pulled off Oliver's cap and threw it into a corner. Then, taking him by the shoulder, sat himself down by the table and stood the boy in front of him.

"Now, first, do you know what this is?" asked Sikes, taking up a pistol which lay on the table.

Oliver replied that he did.

"Well," said Sikes, grasping Oliver's wrist and putting the pistol close to his temple. "If you speak a word when you're out of doors with me, except when I speak to you, that loading will be in your head without notice."

So saying, Sikes ordered Oliver to lie down and sleep until they were ready to leave. Oliver stretched himself in his clothes on a mattress on the floor. Nancy, putting wood on the fire, sat before it in readiness to wake them at the appointed time.

When Oliver awoke, Sikes was thrusting various articles into the pockets of his great-coat, which hung over the back of a chair. Nancy was busily preparing breakfast. It was not yet daylight, for the candle was still burning and it was quite dark outside. A sharp rain, too, was beating against the windowpanes, and the sky looked black and cloudy.

Nancy, scarcely looking at Oliver, threw him a handkerchief to tie around his throat. Sikes gave him a large, rough cape to button over his shoulders. Sikes then clasped Oliver's hand firmly in his, and led him away. Oliver turned when they reached the door, in the hope of catching a glance from Nancy. But she had gone to her old seat in front of the fire and sat, perfectly still, before it.

It was a cheerless morning when they got into the street, blowing and raining hard. There appeared to be nobody stirring, the windows of the houses were all closely shut and the streets through which they passed were noiseless and empty. Now and then a stagecoach, covered with mud, rattled briskly by. One by one the shops began to open and people came out into the streets. Labourers going to their work, men and women with fish-baskets on their heads, donkey-carts laden with vegetables, wagons filled with cattle, milk-women with pails.

Sikes and Oliver made their way through the city until they reached the market at Smithfield. Oliver stared in amazement. The ground was covered, nearly ankle-deep, with filth and mire; a thick steam, rising from the bodies of the pigs and cattle and mingling with the fog that seemed to rest upon the chimney-tops, hung heavily above. All the pens in the centre of the large area were filled with sheep. Countrymen, butchers, boys, thieves, and tramps mingled together in a mass.

Sikes, dragging Oliver after him, paid very little attention to

the sights and sounds that astonished the boy. "Come!" he said sharply. "Don't lag behind already, lazy-legs!"

They continued swiftly on their way until they reached the other side of the city, when an empty cart, which was at some little distance behind, came up. Sikes asked the driver, with as much politeness as he could, if he would give them a lift.

"Jump up," said the man.

Sikes helped Oliver into the cart, and the driver, pointing to a heap of sacks, told him to lie down. As they passed the milestones by the side of the road, Oliver wondered more and more where Sikes meant to take him. At length the cart reached the end of its journey and Sikes and Oliver got down to continue on foot. They walked for a long time, passing many large gardens and gentlemen's houses on both sides of the road, until they reached a town. Here, against the wall of a house, Oliver saw written in large letters, "Hampton". Sikes turned into an old public house and ordered some dinner by the kitchen fire. They ate cold meat and sat so long afterwards that Oliver began to feel certain they were not going any farther. Being tired with the walk, he dozed a little, then fell fast asleep.

It was quite dark when he was awakened by a push from Sikes, and they set off once more. The night was very dark. A damp mist rose from the river and the marshy ground about, and spread itself over the fields. It was piercing cold too. They walked on, in mud and darkness, until they came within sight of the lights of another town not far away. Looking ahead, Oliver saw that the water was just below them, and that they were coming to the foot of a bridge.

Sikes kept straight on, then turned suddenly down a bank on the left.

The water! thought Oliver, turning sick with fear. He has brought me to this lonely place to murder me!

He was about to struggle, when he saw that they stood in front of a solitary house, all ruinous and decayed. Sikes, with Oliver's hand still in his, softly approached the low porch and raised the latch. The door opened, and they went in together.

"Hallo!" cried a harsh voice as soon as they set foot in the passage.

"Don't make such a row!" said Sikes, bolting the door. "Show a light, Toby."

"A light," cried the harsh voice. "A light, Barney!"

A pair of feet shuffled hastily across the bare floor, and from a door on the right came first a feeble candle, next a dishevelled-looking man. He spoke through his nose: "Bister Sikes!" exclaimed Barney. "Cub id, sir. Cub id."

Sikes pushed Oliver in front of him and they entered a low dark room with a smoky fire, two or three broken chairs, a table, and a very old couch on which a man was lying, smoking a long clay-pipe.

Toby Crackit was dressed in a smartly cut coat with brass buttons, an orange neckerchief, a coarse waistcoat, and drab breeches. "Hallo!" he exclaimed when he saw Oliver. He sat up and demanded who this was.

"The boy. Only the boy!" replied Sikes.

"Wud of Bister Fagid's lads," exclaimed Barney with a grin.

The three men were soon in busy preparation. Sikes and Crackit covered their necks and chins in large dark shawls; Barney opened a cupboard and brought forth several articles which he hastily crammed into their pockets.

"Pistols for me, Barney," said Crackit. "Rope, keys, lanterns – nothing forgotten?" He fastened a small crowbar to the loop inside his coat.

"Bring them bits of timber, Barney," said Sikes, and he took a thick stick from Barney's hands. "Now then," he said, holding out his hand.

Oliver, who was completely bemused by what he saw, put his hand mechanically into Sikes's. Crackit took Oliver's other hand and together the two robbers and the boy set off, leaving Barney behind.

After walking about a quarter of a mile, they stopped in front of a detached house surrounded by a wall. Toby Crackit, scarcely pausing to take breath, climbed to the top in an instant.

"The boy next," said Crackit. "Hoist him up."

Before Oliver had time to look around, Sikes had caught him under the arms, and in three or four seconds he and Toby were lying on the grass on the other side. Sikes followed, and they crept cautiously towards the house.

And now for the first time Oliver, near mad with terror, saw that housebreaking and robbery, if not murder, were the objects of the expedition.

They reached a little shuttered window. Sikes took the crowbar and set to work. After some delay, the shutter swung open on its hinges.

"Now listen," whispered Sikes to Oliver. "I'm going to put you through there. Take this light, go softly up the steps straight in front of you and along the hall to the street door. Unfasten it, and let us in."

"There's a bolt at the top you won't be able to reach," interrupted Crackit. "Stand on one of the hall chairs."

Crackit then stood firmly with his head against the wall beneath the window, and his hands upon his knees, so as to make a step of his back. Sikes lifted Oliver on to Toby's back and then gently through the window with his feet first, and without leaving hold of his collar, planted him safely on the floor inside.

"Take this lantern," said Sikes. "You see the stairs in front of you?"

"Yes," gasped Oliver.

Sikes, pointing to the street door with the pistol barrel, reminded him that he was within range all the way, and that if he hesitated, he would be shot in an instant.

Suddenly Sikes stopped.

"Listen!" he said in alarm.

"What's that?" whispered Crackit.

They listened intently.

"Nothing," said Sikes, releasing his hold of Oliver. "Now! Go!"

Oliver had firmly resolved that, whether he died in the attempt or not, he would make one effort to dart upstairs and alarm the family. Filled with this idea, he advanced at once, but stealthily.

"Come back!" Sikes suddenly cried aloud. "Back! Back!"

Scared by the sudden noise, Oliver dropped the lantern.

There was a cry, a light appeared, he saw two men at the top of the stairs, a flash, a loud noise, smoke, a crash, and he staggered back towards the window. Sikes had him by the collar before the smoke had cleared away. He fired his own pistol after the men, and dragged Oliver through the window.

"Give me a shawl!" said Sikes. "They've hit him. Quick!"

Then came the loud ringing of a bell, pistol shots, and the shouts of men, and the feeling of being carried quickly over uneven ground. When the noises faded, Oliver felt cold creeping all over him, and he saw and heard no more.

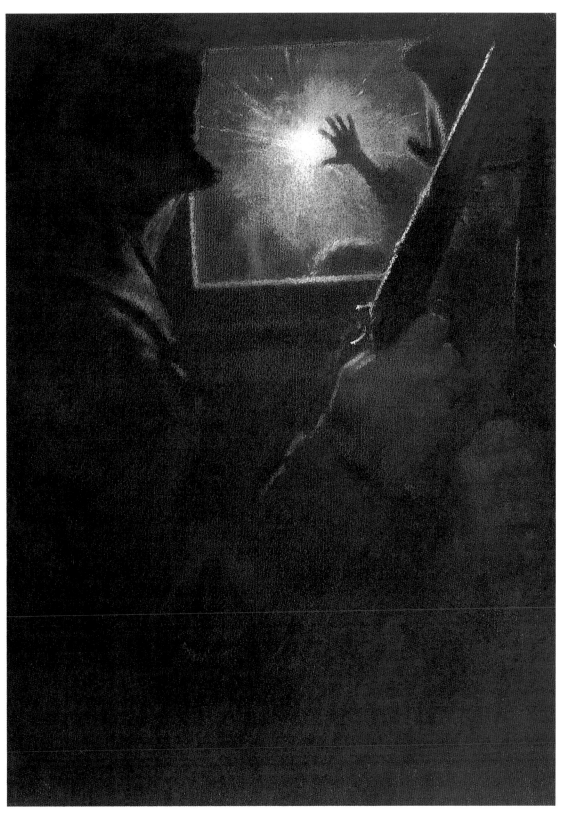

A flash, a loud noise, smoke, a crash, and he staggered back.

CHAPTER 6

The night was bitter cold. The snow lay on the ground, frozen into a thick, hard crust. Indoors, Mrs Corney, widow and matron of the workhouse where Oliver was born, sat herself down in front of a cheerful fire in her little room to enjoy a cup of tea.

She was disturbed by a soft tap at the door and went to open it.

"Oh! Mr Bumble!" said Mrs Corney.

"At your service, ma'am," said the beadle. He rubbed his shoes clean, shook the snow off his coat, and with his cocked hat in his hand, entered the room.

There was a short silence. The beadle coughed. Then Mrs Corney bashfully inquired whether he would like a cup of tea.

In an instant Mr Bumble drew another chair up to the table. As he seated himself, he looked at the lady. She fixed her eyes on the teapot. Mr Bumble coughed again, and smiled slightly.

Mrs Corney went to get another cup and saucer from the cupboard. As she sat down, her eyes once again met those of the gallant beadle. She blushed, and busied herself with making the tea. Again Mr Bumble coughed – louder this time than he had coughed yet.

"Sugar, Mr Bumble?" asked the matron.

"Yes, indeed, ma'am," replied Mr Bumble. He fixed his eyes on Mrs Corney as he said this, and if ever a beadle looked tender, Mr Bumble was that beadle.

They talked for a while – Mr Bumble edging his chair ever so slightly around the table, closer to Mrs Corney. He drank his tea to the last drop, finished a piece of toast, whisked the crumbs off his knee, wiped his lips, and then quite deliberately kissed the matron.

"Mr Bumble!" cried the lady in a whisper, for the shock was so great that she had lost her voice. "Mr Bumble, I shall scream!" Mr Bumble made no reply, but in a slow and dignified manner, put his arm around the matron's waist.

Just as the matron was about to scream, there was a hasty knocking at the door. Mr Bumble darted to the bottles on the cabinet and began dusting them with great purpose.

"If you please, mistress," said an old lady, putting her head in at the door. "Old Mrs Thingummy's going fast."

"Well, so what?" demanded the matron angrily.

"She says she has got something to tell, which you must hear."

Hastily picking up her shawl and asking Mr Bumble to stay till she came back, Mrs Corney followed the old woman from the room. The old woman led her along passages and up some stairs to the room where the sick woman lay. It was a bare attic room, with a dim light burning at the far end. There was another old woman watching by the bed. The matron pushed both old attendants from the room, closed the door, and went to sit at the bedside.

"Come here! Nearer! Let me whisper in your ear!" cried Mrs Thingummy, raising herself from her bed. She clutched the matron by the arm. "Now listen to me. In this very room I once nursed a very pretty girl who was brought in with her feet cut and bruised with walking. She gave birth to a boy, and died."

"What about her?" asked Mrs Corney impatiently.

Mrs Thingummy's face was flushed. "I robbed her, so I did! She wasn't cold – I tell you, she wasn't cold when I stole it!"

"Stole what, for goodness' sake?" cried the matron.

"*It*!" replied the woman. "The only thing she had. It was gold, I tell you. Rich

"Mr Bumble!" cried the lady. "Mr Bumble, I shall scream!"

gold that might have saved her life!"

"Gold!" echoed the matron, bending eagerly over the dying woman. "Go on, go on! What of it! Who was the mother?"

"She told me to keep it safe," replied the woman with a groan. "She trusted me. They would have treated the child better if they had known it all!"

"Known what?" asked the matron. "Speak!"

"The boy grew so like his mother," said Mrs Thingummy, rambling on.

"What was the boy's name?" demanded the matron.

"They *called* him Oliver," replied the woman feebly. "The gold I stole was. . ."

"Yes, yes – what?" cried the other.

But Mrs Thingummy muttered some indistinct sounds in her throat, and fell lifeless on the bed.

* * *

After waiting a considerable while, Mr Bumble began to think that it was time for Mrs Corney to return. He sat, thinking, and then said aloud, "I'll do it!"

Just then Mrs Corney, hurrying into the room, threw herself in a breathless state on a chair by the fireside.

"Mrs Corney!" said Mr Bumble, stooping over the matron. "What is it? Has anything happened, ma'am? I'm on. . . on. . ." Mr Bumble, in his alarm, could not immediately think of the word "tenterhooks", so he said "broken bottles".

"Oh, Mr Bumble," cried the lady. "I've been so dreadfully upset!"

"Upset!" exclaimed Mr Bumble. "Who has dared to. . .?"

"It's dreadful to think of!" said the lady, shuddering.

"Then *don't* think of it, ma'am," rejoined Mr Bumble.

Mrs Corney stopped shaking and the two sat for a while. Mrs Corney sighed.

"Don't sigh, Mrs Corney," said Mr Bumble.

"I can't help it," said Mrs Corney. And she sighed again. Then she placed her hand in Mr Bumble's, and he kissed her.

"The little word?" said Mr Bumble, bending over the bashful Mrs Corney.

67

"The one little, little, little word, my blessed Corney?"

"Ye-ye-yes!" sighed the matron, and threw her arms around him.

"One more," pursued the beadle. "Compose your feelings for only one more. When is it to come off?"

Mrs Corney twice tried to speak, and twice failed. At length summoning up courage, she threw her arms around Mr Bumble's neck, and said it might be as soon as ever he pleased, and that he was an "irresistible duck".

The contract was solemnly ratified with a cupful of peppermint tea. While it was being disposed of, Mrs Corney acquainted Mr Bumble with the old woman's death.

Mr Bumble then inquired what had so upset his dear Mrs Corney.

"It wasn't anything particular," said the lady evasively.

"It must have been something," urged Mr Bumble. "Won't you tell me?"

"Not now. After we're married, dear."

Mr Bumble had to be satisfied with that. Soon afterwards he put on his cocked hat and once again braved the cold wind of the night.

* * *

On the same night Fagin, the Dodger, and Charley Bates sat in Fagin's den. The old man, brooding over a dull, smoky fire, had fallen into deep thought.

"Hark!" cried the Dodger suddenly. "I heard the bell." Picking up the candle, he crept softly down the stairs.

The bell was rung again with some impatience. After a short pause the Dodger reappeared and whispered to Fagin mysteriously.

"What!" cried Fagin. "Alone?"

The Dodger nodded. Fagin bit his fingers and thought for some seconds, as if he dreaded something, and feared to know the worst. At length he raised his head.

"Where is he?" he asked.

The Dodger pointed to the floor above, and made a gesture, as if to leave the room.

"Yes," said Fagin. "Bring him down. Hush! Quiet, Charley! Scarce, scarce!"

The Dodger came back down the stairs, this time followed by a man who, after casting a glance around the room, pulled off the large wrapper which had hidden the lower half of his face, and disclosed the unwashed, unshorn features of Toby Crackit.

Crackit seemed in no hurry to open the conversation. At first Fagin contented himself with patiently watching his face, as if to gain from its expression some clue to the information he brought, but in vain.

Eventually, Crackit spoke.

"First and foremost, Fagin, how's Bill?"

"What!" screamed Fagin, jumping from his seat.

"Why, you don't mean to say. . ." began Crackit, turning pale.

"Mean!" cried Fagin, stamping furiously on the ground. "Where are they? Sikes and the boy? Where are they hiding? Why have they not been here?"

"The robbery failed," said Crackit faintly.

"I know," replied Fagin, tearing a newspaper from his pocket and pointing to it. "What more?"

"They fired and hit the boy. We cut over the fields at the back, with him between us. They gave chase. . ."

"The boy!"

"Bill had him on his back. We stopped to take him between us. His head hung down, and he was cold. They were close upon our heels. . . Every man for himself. . . We parted company, and left the youngster in a ditch. Alive or dead, that's all I know about him."

Fagin stopped to hear no more, but uttering a loud yell, and twining his hand in his hair, rushed from the room, and from the house. He reached the street corner before he began to recover from the effect of Crackit's information, but continued to press onward wildly. He made straight for a certain public house, The Three Cripples. Fagin walked upstairs, and opening the door of a room, looked anxiously about.

The room was lit by two gaslights, and shutters prevented their glare from being visible outside. The ceiling was blackened to prevent its colour from being damaged by the flaring of the lamps, and the place was so full of tobacco smoke that at first it was scarcely possible to see anything more.

"What can I do for you, Mr Fagin?" said the man at the door.

Fagin whispered, "Is *he* here?"

"No," replied the man.

"Will *he* be here tonight?" asked Fagin.

"*Monks*, do you mean?" inquired the man, hesitating.

"Hush!" said Fagin. "Yes."

"Certain," replied the man. "I expected him here before now. If you'll wait ten minutes, he'll be. . ."

"No, no," said Fagin hastily. "Tell him I came here to see him, and that he must come to me tomorrow."

Fagin scurried off and made his way to Bill Sikes's, where he found Nancy, alone, lying with her head on the table. She eyed his crafty face carefully as she asked whether there was any news, and listened to his telling of Toby Crackit's story. When it was over, she sat, saying not a word, tears running down her cheeks.

"And where do you think Bill is now, my dear?" asked Fagin.

Nancy, sobbing, answered that she did not know.

"And the boy too," said Fagin.

"The child," said Nancy, suddenly looking up, "is better where he is, than among us. I hope he lies dead in the ditch, and that his young bones may rot there."

Fagin jumped up in fury, and screamed, "The boy's worth hundreds of pounds to me! He *must* be found!"

Certain that Bill Sikes had not been home, and leaving Nancy sobbing at the table, Fagin departed. It was nearly midnight. He had reached the corner of his own street and was already fumbling in his pocket for the key, when a dark figure emerged from a doorway that lay deep in shadow, and crossing the road, glided up to him unnoticed.

"Fagin!" whispered a voice close to his ear.

"Ah!" said Fagin, turning quickly around. "Is that –"

"Yes," interrupted the stranger. "I've been waiting here for two hours. Where have you been?"

"On your business, my dear," replied Fagin, glancing uneasily at his companion.

"Oh, of course!" said the stranger with a sneer. "Well, and what's come of it?"

"Nothing good," said Fagin.

"Nothing bad, I hope," said the stranger, stopping short and turning with a startled look at Fagin.

Fagin unlocked the door and led the stranger upstairs to the top storey. They talked for some time in whispers. Finally Monks, the stranger, raised his voice a little. "I tell you again, it was badly planned. Why didn't you keep Oliver here and make a pickpocket of him!"

"He was no good. He'd have got caught," wailed Fagin.

Suddenly Monks started. "What's that?" he whispered.

"What!" cried Fagin. "Where!"

"Over there!" replied Monks, glaring at the opposite wall. "The shadow! I saw the shadow of a woman."

Fagin and Monks rushed from the room. The candle, burned down by the draught, was standing where it had been placed. It showed them only the empty staircase. They listened, but could hear nothing.

"You're imagining things," said Fagin, picking up the candle and turning to Monks.

"I know I saw it!" replied Monks, trembling. "It was bending forward when I saw it first, and when I spoke it darted away."

They searched all the rooms, but found no one.

CHAPTER 7

The three men who had been searching the field stopped to discuss what to do next.

"My advice," said the fattest man of the party, "is that we 'mediately go home again."

"I am agreeable to anything which is agreeable to Mr Giles," said a shorter man, who was by no means a slim figure, and who was very pale in the face.

"I shouldn't wish to appear ill-mannered," said the third, who had called the dogs back, "Mr Giles ought to know."

Thus agreed, the men turned back towards the house.

The air grew colder and the mist rolled along the ground like a dense cloud of smoke. The grass was wet; the paths were all mud and water. Still, Oliver lay motionless where Sikes had left him.

At length he awoke and gave out a low cry of pain. His left arm, bandaged in a shawl, hung heavy and useless at his side. The bandage was soaked with blood. Trembling in every joint, he got up and tried to walk. His head was dizzy, but he stumbled onward. He looked about and saw that not far away was a house. He summoned up all his strength and headed towards it.

As he drew nearer, a feeling came over him that he had seen the house before. The shape of the building seemed familiar to him.

That garden wall! Last night he had fallen on his knees on the grass inside. It was the very house they had attempted to rob.

Oliver was so frightened when he recognized the place that for an instant he forgot the agony of his wound and thought only of flight. But he could hardly stand. He pushed against the garden gate; it was unlocked and swung open on its hinges. He staggered across the lawn, climbed the steps, knocked faintly at the door, and sank down against one of the pillars of the portico.

Inside, Mr Giles the butler sat in the kitchen with Mr Brittles the houseboy, the cook, and the housemaid. Mr Giles was recounting how he had shot the intruder and how he and Brittles had given chase. Everyone jumped up at the sound outside, and the housemaid screamed.

"It was a knock," said Mr Giles. "Open the door, somebody."

Brittles went cautiously to the door and opened it. The group, peeping over one another's shoulders, beheld no more formidable sight than poor Oliver.

"A boy!" exclaimed Mr Giles. "What's the matter with the. . . Why, Brittles, look here!"

Brittles no sooner saw Oliver than he gave a loud cry. Mr Giles, seizing the boy by one leg and his good arm, lugged him straight into the hall and deposited him at full length on the floor.

"Here he is!" bawled Giles in great excitement. "Here's one of the thieves, ma'am! Here's a thief, miss! Wounded, miss! I shot him, miss!"

"Giles!" whispered a voice from the top of the stairs.

"I'm here, miss," replied Mr Giles. "Don't be frightened, miss. I ain't much injured. He didn't make a very desperate resistance, miss."

"Hush!" replied the young lady. "You frighten my Aunt. Is the poor creature much hurt?"

"Wounded desperate, miss," replied Giles complacently.

"Wait quietly while I speak to Aunt."

73

With a footstep as soft and gentle as the voice, the speaker left. She soon returned, with the instruction that the wounded person was to be carried carefully upstairs to Mr Giles's room, and that Brittles was to saddle the pony and go instantly into town to fetch the constable and the doctor.

The old servant nodded, then bending over Oliver, helped to carry him upstairs.

Soon a small carriage drove up to the garden gate. A fat gentleman jumped out, ran straight up to the door, and burst into the room, nearly overturning Mr Giles and the breakfast table together.

"I never heard of such a thing!" exclaimed the fat gentleman, Dr Losberne. "My dear Mrs Maylie. . . Bless my soul. . . In the silence of the night too. I never heard of such a thing."

The doctor seemed especially troubled by the fact of the robbery having been unexpected, and attempted in the night time, as if robbers were supposed to arrive at noon, and to make an appointment a day or two before.

"And you, Miss Rose," said the doctor, turning to the young lady, "are you. . ."

"Oh, quite so," said Rose, interrupting him. "But there is a poor creature upstairs, whom Aunt wishes you to see."

"Where is he?" said the doctor. "Show me the way. I'll look in again as I come down, Mrs Maylie."

Talking all the way, he followed Mr Giles upstairs. He was absent much longer than either he or the two ladies had expected. A large, flat box was fetched out of the carriage, and a bedside bell was rung so often that the servants had to run up and down stairs perpetually. It was therefore concluded that something important was going on above. At length the doctor returned, and in reply to an anxious inquiry about his patient, looked very mysterious and closed the door carefully.

"This is a very extraordinary thing, Mrs Maylie," said the doctor. "Have you seen this thief?"

"No," answered the old lady.

"Nor heard anything about him?"

"No."

"I beg your pardon," interrupted Mr Giles, "but I was going to tell you about him when Dr Losberne came in."

The fact was that Mr Giles had not, at first, been able to admit that he had shot only a boy. He had been commended so highly for his bravery that he could not help postponing the explanation for a few minutes.

"Rose wished to see the man," said Mrs Maylie, "but I wouldn't hear of it."

"Humph!" replied the doctor. "There is nothing very alarming in his appearance. Have you any objections to seeing him in my presence?"

"If it be necessary," replied the old lady, "certainly not."

"I am quite sure that you would deeply regret not having done so. He is perfectly quiet and comfortable now."

So saying, the doctor led Miss Rose and Mrs Maylie upstairs. He stepped into the room, and motioning to them to advance, he closed the door when they had entered and gently drew back the curtains of the bed. Upon it, instead of the ruffian they had expected to see, there lay a mere child. His wounded arm, bound and splintered up, was crossed upon his breast; his head reclined upon the other arm.

"What can this mean?" exclaimed the old lady. "This poor child can never have been the pupil of robbers!"

The doctor shook his head in a manner which intimated that he feared it was very possible, and observing that they might disturb the patient, led the way into an adjoining room.

"But even if he has been wicked," pursued Rose, "think how young he is. Think that he may never have known a mother's love, that want of food may have driven him to men who have forced him to crime. Aunt, think of this before you let them drag this sick child to prison. Oh, as you know that I have never felt the want of parents in your goodness and affection, but might have been equally helpless as this poor child, have pity on him!"

"My dear," said the old lady, "do you think I would harm a hair on his head?"

Instead of the ruffian they expected to see, there lay a mere child.

Turning to the doctor, she asked, "What can I do to save him?"

Dr Losberne thrust his hands in his pockets and paced the room, deep in thought.

"I think if you give me full permission to bully Giles and Brittles, I can manage it. I shall persuade Giles that he shot the boy in error. You don't object to that?"

"Unless there is some other way of preserving the child," replied Mrs Maylie.

"There is no other."

"Then my aunt invests you with full power," said Rose.

"The point of my argument is yet to come," continued the doctor. "He will wake in an hour or so. Now, I make this stipulation – that I shall examine him in your presence and that, if from what he says we judge that he is a real and thorough bad one, he shall be handed over to the constable without further interference."

Rose and Mrs Maylie reluctantly agreed and they sat down to wait until Oliver should awake. It was evening before he did so. He recounted his story and none of them were left in any doubt as to his virtuous nature.

Dr Losberne duly went downstairs to speak with Giles and Brittles. They were sitting in the kitchen with the women servants and the constable.

"How is the patient tonight, sir?" asked Giles.

"So-so," returned the doctor. "I am afraid you have got yourself into a scrape there, Mr Giles."

Mr Giles turned pale, as did Mr Brittles.

"Tell me this," said the doctor, addressing them both. "Are you going to take it upon yourselves to swear that that boy upstairs is the boy that was put through the little window last night? Out with it! Come! We are prepared for you!"

The doctor, who was considered one of the best-tempered men on earth, made this demand in such a dreadful tone of anger that Giles and Brittles stared at each other in a state of stupefaction.

"Pay attention to the reply, constable, will you?" said the doctor.

The constable looked as wise as he could, considering the allowance of ale he had just consumed.

"It's a simple matter of identity, you will observe," said the doctor.

"That's what it is, sir," replied the constable, coughing with great violence, for he had finished his ale in a hurry, and some of it had gone the wrong way.

"I ask you again," thundered the doctor to Mr Giles and Mr Brittles, "are you, on your solemn oaths, able to identify the boy?"

Brittles looked doubtfully at Mr Giles; Mr Giles looked doubtfully at Brittles. The good doctor had made his point.

* * *

Cared for by Rose, Mrs Maylie, and Dr Losberne, Oliver began to get better. Often he would tell Rose how grateful he was and ask that he be allowed to work for them to repay their kindness. Rose assured him that the time would come when he would be able to help them in the house and the garden.

"But I was thinking that I am ungrateful now," persisted Oliver.

"To whom?" inquired Rose.

"To the kind gentleman and the dear old nurse who took so much care of me before," answered Oliver. "If they knew how happy I am, they would be pleased, I am sure."

"I am sure they would," replied Rose, "and Dr Losberne has already been kind enough to promise that when you are well enough to go, he will take you to see them."

Oliver's face brightened with pleasure.

In a short time Oliver was sufficiently recovered to undergo the journey. One morning he and Dr Losberne set out in a little carriage that belonged to Mrs Maylie. As Oliver knew the name of the street in which Mr Brownlow lived, they were able to drive straight there. When the carriage turned into it, Oliver's heart was beating so violently, he could hardly breathe.

"Now, my boy, which house is it?" asked Dr Losberne.

"That!" replied Oliver, pointing out of the window. "The White House!"

The doctor patted him on the shoulder. "You will see them directly, and they will be overjoyed to find you safe and well."

The coach rolled on. When it stopped, Oliver looked up at the windows of the house. But the white house was empty, and there was a notice in the window. "To Let."

"Knock at the next door," cried Dr Losberne to the driver, taking hold of Oliver's arm in his. When a servant answered, Dr Losberne called out, "What has become of Mr Brownlow, who used to live in the adjoining house, do you know?"

The servant did not know, but would go and ask. She presently returned and said that Mr Brownlow had sold off his goods and gone to the West Indies, six weeks before.

"Has the housekeeper gone too?" asked Dr Losberne.

"Yes, sir," replied the servant. "The old gentleman, the housekeeper, and a gentleman who was a friend of Mr Brownlow's all went together."

"Then turn towards home again," said Dr Losberne to the driver. "And don't stop till you get out of this confounded London."

This disappointment caused Oliver much sorrow, for he had thought many times of Mr Brownlow and Mrs Bedwin, and their kindness.

A fortnight later, when the fine weather had begun, Rose and Mrs Maylie, accompanied by Dr Losberne, Mr Giles, and Mr Brittles, left their house to spend several months at a cottage in the country, and took Oliver with them. Every morning he would be up by six o'clock, roaming the fields looking for wildflowers, and he went every day to a white-headed old gentleman who taught him to read better, and to write. Then he would walk with Mrs Maylie and Rose and hear them talk of books, or perhaps sit with them while Rose read aloud.

Three months sped by, during which time Oliver came to feel completely at home with Rose and Mrs Maylie.

One beautiful evening Oliver sat at the window, reading. He had been poring over his books for some time, and as the day had been unusually warm, he gradually fell asleep.

Oliver knew perfectly well that he was in his own little room, that his books were lying on the table before him. And yet he was asleep. Suddenly the scene changed, the air became close and confined, and he thought, with terror, that he was in Fagin's house again. There sat Fagin, pointing at him, and whispering to another man who sat beside him.

"Hush, my dear!" he thought he heard Fagin say. "It is he, sure enough."

"He!" the other man seemed to answer. "How could I mistake him?"

The man seemed to say this with such hatred that Oliver woke with fear and started up. There at the window, with eyes peering into the room and meeting his, stood Fagin. And beside him were the scowling features of the very man he thought he had just heard speak.

In an instant they were gone. But they had recognized him, and he them. He stood transfixed for a moment, then leaping from the window into the garden, called loudly for help.

When the household, attracted by Oliver's cries, hurried into the garden, they found him pointing in the direction of the fields behind the house and shouting, "Fagin! Fagin!" A search was made, but it was all in vain. There were not even the traces of recent footsteps to be seen.

"They went that way?" asked Dr Losberne. "Are you sure?"

"As I am that the men were at the window," replied Oliver, pointing to the hedge which divided the garden from the field. "The tall man leaped over, just there; and Fagin crept through that gap."

Dr Losberne watched Oliver's earnest face and believed what he said. Still, in no direction were there any appearances of the trampling of men. The grass was long, but nowhere was it trodden down. The sides of the ditches were muddy, but in no place could they discern any footprints. A few days later, with no evidence found, the incident was all but forgotten.

CHAPTER 8

Mr Bumble sat in the workhouse parlour with his eyes moodily fixed on the empty grate. Occasionally he would heave a deep sigh, while a more sombre, gloomy shadow spread across his face. Mr Bumble was no longer a beadle.

Mr Bumble had married Mrs Corney and was master of the workhouse. Another beadle had come into power.

"And tomorrow two months since I was married!" said Mr Bumble with a sigh. "It seems an age. No more than two months ago, I was not only my own master, but everybody else's, so far as the workhouse was concerned, and now. . .!"

It was too much. Mr Bumble got up and walked, distractedly, into the street. He walked up one street, and down another. He felt thirsty and paused before a public house, which was deserted except for one solitary customer. Mr Bumble entered, and ordering something to drink, sat down.

The man who was seated there was tall and dark, and wore a large cloak. He eyed Bumble as he entered, but scarcely deigned to nod his head in acknowledgment.

Mr Bumble sat reading his paper, but every now and then could not resist stealing a look at the stranger. Whenever he did so, he looked away in some confusion, for every time the stranger was also stealing a look at him. When they had encountered each other's glance several times, the stranger, in a deep, harsh voice, broke the silence.

"Were you looking for me," he said, "when you peered in at the window?"

"Not that I am aware of," replied Mr Bumble.

Another silence followed, which was broken again by the stranger.

"I have seen you before, I think?" he said. "You were differently dressed at the time, but I should know you again. You were beadle here, once, were you not?"

"I was," said Mr Bumble in surprise.

"What are you now?" asked the stranger.

"Master of the workhouse," answered Mr Bumble slowly and impressively.

"Now, listen to me," said the stranger. "I came here today to find you. By chance, you walked into the very room I was sitting in. I want some information from you. I don't ask you to give it for nothing. Take this, to begin with."

As he spoke, he pushed a couple of sovereigns across the table. When Mr Bumble had examined the coins to see that they were genuine, and had put them, with much satisfaction, in his waistcoat pocket, the stranger went on:

"Cast your mind back, let me see, twelve years last winter."

"It's a long time," said Mr Bumble. "Good. I've done it."

"The scene, the workhouse."

"Good!"

"And the time, night."

"Yes."

"A boy was born."

"Many boys," observed Mr Bumble, shaking his head.

"I speak of one, a pale-faced boy, who was apprenticed down here to a coffin-maker, and who afterwards ran away to London."

"Why you mean Oliver! Oliver Twist!" said Mr Bumble. "I remember him, of course. There wasn't a worse rascal. . ."

"It's not of him I want to hear. I've heard enough of him," said the stranger, stopping Mr Bumble. "It's of a woman, the woman who nursed his mother. Where is she?"

"She died last winter," answered Mr Bumble.

The man looked hard at him, and then he seemed lost in thought. After a few moments he remarked that it was not important, and got up, as if to leave.

But Mr Bumble was cunning enough, and he at once saw that an opportunity was opened for the lucrative disposal of some secret in the possession of Mrs Bumble. He remembered the night of old Mrs Thingummy's death. Although his wife had never confided to him the secret of which she had been the only witness, he had heard enough to know that it related to something that had occurred while the old woman had attended the mother of Oliver Twist. Hurriedly he informed the stranger, with an air of mystery, that one woman had been with the old woman shortly before she died, and that she could, he believed, throw some light on the subject of his inquiry.

"How can I find her?" asked the stranger.

"Only through me," answered Mr Bumble.

"When?" cried the stranger hastily.

"Tomorrow," replied Bumble.

"At nine in the evening," said the stranger, producing a scrap of paper and writing on it an address by the waterside. "Bring her to me there. I needn't tell you to be secret."

On glancing at the paper, Mr Bumble noticed that it contained no name.

"What name am I to ask for?"

"Monks," snapped the man, and strode hastily away.

* * *

It was a wet summer evening when Mr and Mrs Bumble, turning out of the main street of the town, made their way to a cluster of ruined houses next to the river. They were both wrapped in old and shabby coats, which protected them from the rain, and also sheltered them from being recognized.

Mr and Mrs Bumble stopped in front of a large, dilapidated building. "The place should be somewhere here," said Bumble, looking at the scrap of paper in his hand.

"Hallo there!" cried a voice from above.

Mr Bumble raised his head and saw a man looking out of a door on the second storey.

"Stand still a minute," cried the voice. "I'll be with you directly." The head disappeared and the door closed.

"Is that the man?" asked Mrs Bumble.

Mr Bumble nodded.

"Then do as I told you," snapped the wife, "and be careful to say as little as you can, or you'll give us away at once."

Monks opened a small door, and beckoned them in.

"This is the woman, is it?" he demanded.

"That is the woman," replied Mr Bumble.

"Now," said Monks, when they had all seated themselves, "she knows what I'm after, does she?"

The question was directed at Mr Bumble, but his wife anticipated the reply by indicating that she was perfectly acquainted with the matter. Monks then spoke to her directly.

"This man is right in saying that you were with the old woman the night she died, and that she told you something. . ."

"About the mother of the boy you named," replied Mrs Bumble, interrupting him. "Yes."

"The first question is, what did she say?"

"That's the second question," said Mrs Bumble with much deliberation. "The first is, what is the information worth?"

"How can I tell that, without knowing what it is?" cried Monks.

"You had better make an offer," replied Mrs Bumble calmly.

"Twenty pounds," said Monks.

"Twenty-five. Give me twenty-five pounds in gold," said the matron, "and I'll tell you all I know. Not before."

Monks hesitated only a moment then thrust a hand into a side pocket, and producing a canvas bag, counted out twenty-five sovereigns on the table and pushed them over to the woman.

"Now," he said, "let's hear your story."

The thunder having subsided, Monks bent forward to listen to what Mrs Bumble had to say. The faces of the three nearly touched, as the two men leaned over the small table in their eagerness to hear, and Mrs Bumble also leaned forward to make herself heard.

"When this woman, that we called Mrs Thingummy, was dying," began Mrs Bumble, "she spoke of a young woman who had given birth to a child some years before. The child was the one you talked of to my husband last night. . ."

"Go on!" whispered Monks.

"After his mother had died, Mrs Thingummy stole from her something she had begged her to keep for the child's sake."

"She stole it?" cried Monks eagerly. "Did she sell it? Where? When? To whom?"

"As soon as she had told me that she had done this," said Mrs Bumble, "she fell back and died."

"Without saying more?" cried Monks. "It's a lie! She said more! Tell me what she said!"

"She didn't utter another word," said the matron, "but she clutched my gown violently with one hand, and when I saw that she was dead, and removed the hand, I found it held a scrap of dirty paper."

"Which contained. . ." interrupted Monks.

"Nothing," replied the woman. "It was a pawnbroker's ticket."

"For what?"

"I imagine she had pawned it and had scraped together money to pay the pawnbroker's interest year by year, and prevent its running out, so that if anything came of it, it could still be redeemed. Nothing had come of it and she died with the scrap of paper in her hand. I thought something might one day come of it too, and so I redeemed the pledge."

"Where is it now?"

"There," replied the woman. And she threw upon the table a small leather bag, which Monks pounced upon and

85

tore open with trembling hands. It contained a little gold locket, in which were two locks of hair, and a plain gold wedding ring.

"It has the word 'Agnes' engraved on the inside," said Mrs Bumble.

"And this is all?" said Monks after looking at the locket closely.

"All," replied the woman.

Mr Bumble drew a long breath, as if he were glad to find that the story was over, and now plucked up courage to wipe off the perspiration which had been trickling over his nose.

"Is that what you expected of me?" asked Mrs Bumble.

"It is," replied Monks.

"What do you propose to do with it? Can it be used against me?"

"Never," rejoined Monks. "Nor against me either. See here!"

With these words he suddenly wheeled the table aside, and pulling an iron ring in the boarding, threw back a large trapdoor that opened close at Mr Bumble's feet, and caused him to retire several paces backwards with great speed.

"Look down," said Monks, lowering the lantern into the gulf. "Don't fear me. I could have let you down, quietly enough, when you were seated over it, if that had been my game."

Mrs Bumble drew near to the brink, and even Mr Bumble, impelled by curiosity, ventured to do the same. The turbid water, swollen by heavy rain, was rushing rapidly below. Monks drew the little packet from his breast, where he had hurriedly thrust it, and tying it to a leaden weight, dropped it into the stream. It fell straight, hit the water with a scarcely audible splash, and was gone.

"There!" said Monks. "Now light your lantern! And get away from here as fast as you can."

Mr Bumble lit his lantern and went down the stairs in silence, followed by his wife. Monks brought up the rear. They crossed the room below slowly, for Monks jumped at every shadow, and Mr Bumble, holding his lantern a foot above the ground, walked with care, looking nervously about him for hidden trapdoors. The gate was softly unfastened by Monks, and the married couple went out into the wet and darkness.

Monks drew the little packet from his breast and dropped it into the stream.

CHAPTER 9

The following night, Bill Sikes was lying on his bed, wrapped in his great-coat. He looked ill. Bull's-eye sat at the bedside, eyeing his master with a wistful look. Seated by the window, patching an old waistcoat, was Nancy.

"What time is it?" growled Sikes.

"Not long gone seven," said Nancy. "How do you feel tonight, Bill?"

"As weak as water," replied Sikes. "Here, lend us a hand, and let me get off this bed."

"What's the matter, here, my dear?" said Fagin, walking in followed by the Dodger and Charley Bates.

"And where have *you* been?" growled Sikes angrily. "What have you got to say for yourself, you withered old miser?"

"I was away from London a week and more," replied Fagin.

"And what about the other fortnight?" demanded Sikes.

"I couldn't help it, Bill. I couldn't help it."

"That's all very well," said Sikes, "but I must have some money. Tonight."

"I haven't a coin on me," replied Fagin.

"Then you've got lots at home," retorted Sikes. "And I must have some from there."

"Well, well," sighed Fagin. "I'll send the Dodger around presently."

"You won't do anything of the kind," replied Sikes. "Nancy shall go and fetch it." After a great deal of haggling and squabbling, Fagin beat down the amount required from five pounds to three pounds four shillings and sixpence, and returned home, accompanied by Nancy and the boys.

In due course they arrived at Fagin's house. The Dodger and Charley were ordered to bed and as soon as they had gone, Fagin went to get Nancy the money. He was just about to give it to her, when he heard a sound. Laying a forefinger to his lip, Fagin carried a candle to the door as a man's step was heard upon the stairs. He reached it just as the visitor walked in.

It was Monks.

"Only one of my young people," said Fagin, noticing that Monks immediately drew back on seeing Nancy.

"Any news?" asked Fagin.

"Not bad. Let me have a word with you."

Nancy drew closer to the table and made no offer to leave the room, although she could see that Monks was pointing to her. Fagin pointed upward, and took Monks away. Saying something that she could not make out, he seemed, by the creaking of the boards, to lead his companion to the top storey.

Before the sound of their footsteps had ceased to echo through the house, Nancy had slipped off her shoes, and drawing her gown loosely over her head and muffling her arms in it, stood at the door listening with breathless interest. The very moment the noise had ceased, she glided from the room, climbed the stairs silently, and was lost in the darkness above.

After a quarter of an hour the girl glided back swiftly, and immediately afterwards the two men were heard descending. Monks left at once, and Fagin crawled upstairs again for the money. When he returned, Nancy was putting on her shawl and bonnet, as if getting ready to leave.

"Why, Nancy," exclaimed Fagin, "how pale you are! What have you been doing to yourself?"

"Nothing that I know of except sitting in this airless place," replied Nancy carelessly. "Come! Let me get back, please, Fagin."

With a sigh for every piece of money, Fagin counted out the coins into her hand.

When Nancy got into the open street, she sat down upon a doorstep and seemed for a few moments wholly bewildered and unable to go any farther. Suddenly she arose and hurried back to Sikes.

If she betrayed any agitation when she arrived, Sikes did not notice it; he merely asked if she had brought the money, and being told that she had, uttered a growl of satisfaction and went back to sleep.

The next day Nancy was nervous and distracted. When night came, her excitement increased so that even Sikes observed it.

"Why! You look like a corpse come to life again. What's the matter?" he asked.

"Matter!" replied Nancy. "Nothing!"

Sikes drained his glass to the bottom, and then with many grumbling oaths called for his medicine. Nancy jumped up and poured it quickly out, but with her back towards him. Then she held the glass to his lips, while he drank off the contents.

"Now," said Sikes, "come and sit aside of me, and put on your own face; or I'll alter it so that you won't know it again when you *do* want it."

Nancy obeyed. Sikes, locking her hand in his, fell back upon the pillow. His grasp finally relaxed, and he lay like one in a profound trance.

"The laudanum has taken effect at last," murmured the girl as she watched

Sikes. "I may be too late, even now!"

She hastily dressed herself in her bonnet and shawl. She looked fearfully around from time to time, as if, despite the sleeping draught, she expected every moment to feel Sikes's heavy hand upon her shoulder. Then, opening and closing the door noiselessly, she hurried from the house. The clock struck ten, increasing her impatience. She tore along the narrow pavement, until she reached the wealthier part of the city.

She stopped outside a hotel in a quiet, wide street near Hyde Park, hesitated a moment, then walked into the hall. She looked around uncertainly, and made towards the stairs.

"Now, young woman!" said a smartly dressed lady, looking out from a door behind her. "Who do you want here?"

"A lady who is staying in this hotel," answered Nancy.

"What lady?" asked the woman with a scornful look.

"Miss Maylie," said Nancy. "She has not long arrived here from the country."

The young woman, having noted Nancy's appearance, looked disdainfully at her and summoned a waiter to deal with her. Nancy repeated her request.

"Come! Take yourself off," said the waiter, pushing Nancy towards the door.

"I shall be carried out, if I go!" cried Nancy. "Isn't there anyone here that will take a message from me?"

A good-tempered looking cook now stepped forward.

"Take the message up for her, Joe," said the cook.

"What's it to be?" asked the waiter reluctantly.

"That a young woman earnestly asks to speak to Miss Maylie alone," said Nancy.

The man ran upstairs, but soon returned requesting that Nancy follow him to a small anteroom, where he left her.

After a few minutes Nancy looked up to see a beautiful young lady standing before her.

"I am very sorry if anyone has behaved harshly to you," said Rose. "Tell me why you wished to see me. I am the person you asked for."

The kind tone of Rose's answer took Nancy completely by surprise, and she burst into tears.

"Sit down," said Rose gently. "If you are in trouble, I shall be glad to help you if I can. Sit down."

"Let me stand," said Nancy, still weeping, "and do not speak to me so kindly until you know me better. Is. . . is. . . that door shut?"

"Yes," said Rose. "Why?"

"Because," said Nancy, "I am about to put my life, and the lives of others, in your hands. I am the girl that dragged Oliver back to old Fagin's on the night he went out from Mr Brownlow's house."

"You!" said Rose.

"Yes. But I have escaped from those who would surely murder me if they knew I had been here, to tell you what I have overheard. Do you know a man named Monks?"

"No," said Rose.

"He knows you," said Nancy, "and knew you were here, for it was by hearing him tell the place that I found you out.

"Some time ago, and soon after Oliver was put into your house on the night of the robbery, I, suspecting this man, listened to a conversation held between him and Fagin in the dark. I found out from what I heard that Monks had seen Oliver accidentally with two of our boys on the day when we first lost him, and had known him straightaway to be the child that he was looking for. A deal was struck with Fagin, and if Oliver was got back, Fagin should have a certain sum, and he was to have more for making Oliver a thief, which this Monks wanted for some reason of his own."

"For what reason?" asked Rose.

"He caught sight of my shadow on the wall as I listened, in the hope of finding out, and I had to escape. I saw no more of him till last night."

"And what happened then?"

"Last night he came up again. Again Fagin and he went upstairs, and I, wrapping myself up so that my shadow should not betray me, again listened at

"I am about to put my life, and the lives of others, in your hands."

the door. The first words I heard Monks say were these: 'So the only proofs of the boy's identity lie at the bottom of the river, and the old woman that received them from the mother is in her coffin.' They laughed and Monks said that he had got Oliver's money safely now."

"What's all this!" said Rose.

"The truth, lady," replied Nancy. "Then he said that if he could kill Oliver without being caught, he would; but as he couldn't, he'd make sure he'd do him as much harm as he could. 'Fagin,' he said, 'you'll never imagine the traps I'll lay for my young brother, Oliver.'"

"His brother!" exclaimed Rose.

"Those were his words," said Nancy, glancing uneasily around, as she had scarcely ceased to do since she began to speak, for she was haunted by the thought that Sikes had followed her. "It's growing late, and I have to reach home without suspicion of having been on such an errand as this. I must get back quickly."

"But what can I do?" asked Rose. "This mystery must be investigated, or how will its disclosure to me benefit Oliver?"

"You must have some kind gentleman about you that will hear it as a secret, and advise you what to do," replied Nancy.

"But where can I find you again when it is necessary?" asked Rose.

"Will you promise me that you will have my secret strictly kept, and come alone, or with the only other person who knows it; and that I shall not be watched or followed?" asked Nancy.

"I promise," said Rose.

"Every Sunday night, from eleven until the clock strikes twelve," said Nancy, "I shall walk on London Bridge if I am alive."

Nancy then turned away and left the room, while Rose, overpowered by what she had just heard, sank into a chair and tried to collect her thoughts. She felt she had no one in whom she could confide. Dr Losberne was with them, but she was too well acquainted with his impetuosity and wrath to trust him with the secret. For the same reasons, she could not tell her aunt, whose first impulse would be to discuss the matter with the doctor.

Rose spent a sleepless and anxious night. The following morning she was sitting, about to write a letter, when Oliver, who had been out walking with Mr Giles for a bodyguard, ran into the room.

"What makes you look so flurried?" asked Rose.

"I hardly know how to say it," replied Oliver. "To think that I should see him at last, and you should be able to know that I have told you all the truth!"

"I never thought you had told us anything but the truth," said Rose, calming him. "But what is this? Of whom do you speak?"

"I have seen the gentleman!" replied Oliver. "The gentleman who was so good to me, Mr Brownlow!"

"Where?" asked Rose.

"Getting out of a coach," replied Oliver, "and going into a house. I didn't speak to him; I was too nervous. But Giles asked whether he lived there, and they said he did. Look," said Oliver, opening a scrap of paper, "here it is, here's where he lives. I'm going there straightaway."

Rose read the address. "Quick!" she said. "Tell them to fetch the coach and be ready to go with me. I will take you there directly. I will only tell my aunt that we are going out for an hour."

In a little more than five minutes they were on their way to Mr Brownlow's house. When they arrived, Rose left Oliver in the coach, under the pretence of preparing Mr Brownlow to receive him, and sending up her card by the servant, asked to see Mr Brownlow on very urgent business. The servant soon returned, to ask that she go upstairs. Following him into an upper room, Rose was presented to a kindly looking elderly gentleman. Next to him was seated another old gentleman who did not look particularly kindly.

"Mr Brownlow, I believe," said Rose to the kindly looking gentleman.

"That is my name," said the old gentleman. "This is my friend Mr Grimwig. Grimwig, will you leave us for a few minutes?"

"I believe," interrupted Rose, "that, if I have been correctly informed, he knows of the business on which I wish to speak to you."

Mr Brownlow nodded. Mr Grimwig, who had made one very stiff bow and got up from the chair, made another very stiff bow and sat down again.

"I shall surprise you very much, I have no doubt," said Rose, "but you once showed great benevolence and goodness to a very dear friend of mine, and I am sure you will be interested to hear of him again."

"Indeed!" said Mr Brownlow.

"Oliver Twist you knew him as," replied Rose.

Mr Grimwig, who had been pretending to dip into a large book, dropped it with a crash, and let out a long, deep whistle.

Mr Brownlow was no less surprised, although he did not show it.

"Do me the favour, my dear young lady, to leave entirely out of the question that goodness and benevolence of which you speak, and if you have it in your power to produce any evidence which will alter the unfavourable opinion I was once induced to entertain of that poor child, put me in possession of it."

"A bad one! I'll eat my head if he is not a bad one," growled Mr Grimwig.

"Oliver is a child of noble nature and a warm heart," said Rose, blushing.

"Will you tell me what you know of this poor child?" asked Mr Brownlow.

Rose at once told of all that had befallen Oliver since he left Mr Brownlow's house, reserving Nancy's information for that gentleman's ear alone.

"This is great happiness to me," said Mr Brownlow. "Great happiness. But you have not told me where he is now, Miss Maylie. Why have you not brought him?"
"He is waiting in a coach at the door," replied Rose.

"At this door!" cried Mr Brownlow, and hurried out of the room, down the stairs, up the coach steps, and into the coach without another word.

Mr Brownlow soon returned, accompanied by Oliver, whom Mr Grimwig received very graciously.

"There is somebody else who should not be forgotten," said Mr Brownlow, ringing the bell. "Send Mrs Bedwin here, if you please."

The old housekeeper answered the summons with all dispatch, and dropping a curtsy at the door, waited for orders.

"Why, you get blinder every day, Bedwin," said Mr Brownlow.

"Well, that I do, sir," replied Mrs Bedwin. "People's eyes at my time of life don't improve with age, sir."

"Put on your glasses, and see if you can't find out what you were wanted for."

The old lady began to rummage in her pocket for her spectacles. But Oliver's patience ran out, and he sprang into her arms.

"My dear old nurse!" he cried.

"He would come back, I knew he would," said the old lady, holding him in her arms. "How well he looks, and how like a gentleman's son he is dressed again! Where have you been this long time?"

Leaving Mrs Bedwin and Oliver to talk, Mr Brownlow led the way into another room and there heard Rose's full story of her meeting with Nancy. Rose also explained why she did not feel she could confide in Dr Losberne. Mr Brownlow agreed to come to the hotel at eight o'clock that evening to explain things to the doctor, and in the meantime Rose should tell her aunt of all that had happened.

That evening Mr Brownlow, Rose, Dr Losberne, and Mrs Maylie sat together.

"It is quite clear that we shall have extreme difficulty in getting to the bottom of this mystery, unless we can catch this man Monks," said Mr Brownlow. "Before we can resolve any precise course of action, we must see the girl Nancy, to ascertain from her whether she will point out this Monks, on the understanding that he is to be dealt with by us, and not by the law. She cannot be seen until next Sunday night; this is Tuesday. I would suggest that in the meantime we remain perfectly quiet, and keep these matters secret even from Oliver himself.

"Come! Supper has been announced, and young Oliver, who is all alone in the next room, will have begun to think by this time that we have tired of his company."

With these words the old gentleman gave his hand to Mrs Maylie and escorted her into the supper room. Dr Losberne followed, leading Rose, and the meeting was, for the moment, broken up.

CHAPTER 10

On the night when Nancy, having drugged Sikes to sleep, hurried to see Rose Maylie, there came towards London two people – Noah Claypole and Charlotte.

"Where do you mean to stop for the night, Noah?" asked Charlotte.

"How should I know," replied Noah, whose temper had been considerably impaired by walking.

"Near, I hope," said Charlotte.

"No, not near," replied Noah. "A fine thing it would be, wouldn't it, to go and stop at the very first inn we found, so that Sowerberry, if he came after us, might find us and have us taken back in a cart with handcuffs on! No, I shall go and lose myself among the narrowest streets I can find. If it hadn't been for me, and if we hadn't left when we did, you'd have been locked up hard and fast by now."

"Don't put all the blame on me, and say *I* should have been locked up. You would have been if I had been."

"You took the money from the till!" said Noah.

"I took it for you, Noah, dear," replied Charlotte.

"Yes, but you kept it," said Noah, and on he went, without halting. "Now then! Keep close at my heels, and come along." He did not add that he had trusted the money to Charlotte in order that if they were pursued, it might be found on her, leaving him an opportunity of asserting his innocence of any theft.

The two made their way through narrow streets until Noah stopped in

front of an inn, more humble in appearance and more dirty than any he had yet seen, and announced his intention of staying there for the night.

"What's the name of this place?" he asked Charlotte. "T-h-r, three what?"

"Cripples," said Charlotte.

"And a very good sign too." He pushed the door with his shoulder, and entered, followed by Charlotte.

Spying from a back room, Fagin watched as the two ordered something to eat and drink. He listened attentively while they spoke. "Aha!" he whispered. "I like that fellow's looks. He'd be of use to us." And he went out to join them.

Noah looked up. Fagin made a very low bow and set himself down at the nearest table.

"A pleasant night, sir, but cool for the time of year," said Fagin. "From the country, I see, sir?"

"How do you see that?" asked Noah.

"From the dust on your shoes," replied Fagin. "We have not so much dust as that in London." He lifted his glass.

"Good stuff that," observed Noah, smacking his lips.

"A man need be always emptying a till, or a pocket, or a bank, if he drinks it regularly."

Noah looked from Fagin to Charlotte with a countenance of ashy paleness and terror.

"Don't mind me, my dear," said Fagin. "It was lucky it was only me that heard you by chance. It was very lucky it was only me. I'm in that way myself, and I like you for it."

Noah looked at Fagin suspiciously.

"I think I can put you in the right way, where you can take whatever department of the business you think will suit you best at first, and be taught all the others."

"What's the wages?" asked Noah.

"Live like a gentleman, board and lodging, half of all you earn, and half of all the young woman earns," replied Fagin.

Noah might have objected, but he remembered that if he refused, it was in the power of his new acquaintance to give him up to the justice immediately. So he accepted Fagin's offer.

"What business d'you think might suit me?" he asked.

"I heard you talk of something in the spy way, my dear," said Fagin.

"I shouldn't mind turning my hand to it sometimes," answered Noah, "but it wouldn't pay by itself, you know. Perhaps something in the way of stealing?"

Noah and Fagin concluded their deal. It was agreed that Noah and Charlotte should meet Fagin at his house at ten o'clock the next morning. After saying good night, Fagin left.

The following day, when Noah and Charlotte arrived at Fagin's rooms, they found Fagin in an anxious state.

"My best man has been taken from me!" Fagin exclaimed.

"You don't mean to say he died?" asked Noah.

"No, no," replied Fagin. "Not as bad as that. Wanted. He was wanted. He was charged with attempting to pick a pocket, and they found a silver snuffbox on him. They remanded him till today, for they thought they knew the owner. You should have known the Dodger, my dear, you should have known the Dodger."

"Well, I shall know him, I hope, don't you think?" said Noah.

"I'm doubtful about it," replied Fagin with a sigh. "If they don't get any fresh evidence, it'll only be a summary conviction, and we shall have him back again after six weeks or so; but if they do, he'll be transported for life."

Just then Charley Bates came in, with his hands in his pockets and his face twisted into a look of semi-comical woe.

"It's all up, Fagin," said Charley, when he had been introduced to Noah and Charlotte. "They've found the gentleman who owns the box; two or three more's coming to identify the Dodger."

"We must know how he gets on in court today," said Fagin. "Let me think."

"Shall I go?" asked Charley.

"Not for the world," replied Fagin. "Are you mad, my dear, that you'd walk into the very place where. . . No, Charley, no. One is enough to lose at a time."

"Then why don't you send *him*," said Charley, pointing at Noah.

"Oh, I don't know about that," replied Noah, backing towards the door and shaking his head. "No, no, none of that. It's not my department, that ain't."

It took some time for Fagin to persuade Noah that he incurred no possible danger in visiting the court. If he were properly disguised, it would be as safe a spot for him to visit as any in London. At length Noah consented, with very bad grace. By Fagin's directions he substituted his own smock, breeches and leggings for a felt hat and a carter's whip.

After he had been told how to recognize the Dodger, he was led by Charley Bates through dark and winding streets to within a short distance of Bow Street. Having described where the court was, Charley Bates told him to hurry on alone, and promised to wait for him.

Noah reached the court, where he found himself jostled among a crowd of people. They were huddled together in a dirty room at the upper end of which was a raised platform railed off from the rest, with a dock for the prisoners on the left hand against the wall, a table for barristers in the middle, and a desk for the magistrates on the right.

Noah looked eagerly about him for the Dodger, but saw nobody at all answering to his description. He waited in a state of much uncertainty until the case in progress was over, and then was relieved by the appearance of another prisoner who he felt at once could be no other than the Dodger.

It was indeed the Dodger who, shuffling into the office with the big coat sleeves tucked up as usual, his left hand in his pocket and his hat in his right hand, preceded the jailer, and taking his place in the dock, requested in a loud voice what he was placed in "this 'ere disgraceful situation for."

"Hold your tongue, will you?" said the jailer.

"I'm an Englishman, ain't I?" answered the Dodger. "Where are my privileges?"

"I'm an Englishman, ain't I?" answered the Dodger. "Where are my privileges?"

"You'll get your privileges soon enough," retorted the jailer.

"We'll see wot the Secretary of State for the Home Affairs has got to say to the police, if I don't," replied the Dodger. "Now then! Wot is this here business? I shall thank the madg'strates to dispose of this here little affair, and not to keep me while they read the paper, for I've got an appointment with a genelman in the City, and as I'm a man of my word and wery punctual in business matters, he'll go away if I ain't there to my time."

"Silence there!" cried the jailer.

"What is this?" asked one of the magistrates.

"A pickpocketing case, your worship."

"Has the boy ever been here before?"

"He ought to have been, a many times," replied the jailer. "*I* know him well, your worship."

"Oh! You know me, do you?" cried the Dodger. "Wery good. That's a case of deformation of character, anyway."

There was a laugh from the crowd, and a cry of silence from the clerk.

"Now then, where are the witnesses?" asked the clerk.

A policeman stepped forward who had seen the Dodger attempt to pick the pocket of an unknown gentleman in the crowd, and indeed take a handkerchief, which, being a very old one, he deliberately put back again. For this reason he took the Dodger into custody as soon as he could get near him, and the Dodger, being searched, had upon him a silver snuffbox, with the owner's name engraved upon the lid. This gentleman had been found and swore that the snuffbox was his, and that he had missed it on the previous day, the moment he had left the crowd before referred to. He had also noticed a young gentleman in the throng, and that young gentleman was the prisoner before him.

"Have you anything to ask this witness, boy?" asked the magistrate.

"I wouldn't abase myself by descending to hold no conversation with him," replied the Dodger.

"Have you anything to say at all?"

"No," replied the Dodger, "not here. Besides which my attorney is a-breakfasting this morning with the Wice President of the House of Commons, but I shall have something to say elsewhere, and so will he, and so will a wery numerous and 'spectable circle of acquaintances as'll make them police wish they'd never been born. I'll –"

"There! He's fully committed!" interrupted the clerk. "Take him away!"

The Dodger was led off by the collar, threatening, till he got into the yard. He was then locked in a cell.

Noah, having seen him locked up by himself, made his way back to where he had left Charley Bates, and the two hurried back to tell Fagin the news.

CHAPTER 11

It was a Sunday night, and the bell of the nearest church struck the hour. Sikes and Fagin were talking, but they paused to listen. Eleven.

"An hour this side of midnight," said Sikes, raising the blind to look out and returning to his seat. "Dark and heavy it is too. A good night for business, this."

Fagin, pulling Sikes by the sleeve, pointed his finger towards Nancy, who was putting on her bonnet, and was now leaving the room.

"Nancy!" cried Sikes. "Where are you going at this time of night?"

"Not far."

"What answer's that?" replied Sikes. "Where are you going?"

"I don't know where," replied Nancy.

"Then I do," said Sikes obstinately. "Nowhere. Sit down!"

"I'm not well. I want a breath of air," said Nancy.

"Put your head out of the window," replied Sikes.

"There's not enough there," said Nancy. "I want it in the street."

"Then you won't have it," replied Sikes. With which he rose, locked the door, took the key out, and pulling her bonnet from her head, flung it on top of an old cupboard. "There," he said. "Now stop quietly where you are, will you?"

"Let me go," said Nancy, pleading. Then sitting herself down on the floor before the door, she said, "Bill, let me go. You don't know what you're doing. For only an hour – do – do!"

Sikes seized her roughly by the arm. "If I don't think the girl's gone mad.

Get up!"

"Not till you let me go – not till you let me go – never – never!" screamed Nancy.

Sikes, suddenly pinioning her hands, dragged her, struggling and wrestling with him, into a small room, where he sat himself on a bench, and thrusting her into a chair, held her down by force. She struggled and implored by turns until twelve o'clock had struck, and then, exhausted, ceased to fight any longer.

Fagin sat, deep in thought, in the next room. As soon as Nancy had calmed down, he got up and left, still thoughtful. He had the idea that Nancy, tired of Sikes's brutality, had found some new friend. Her changed manner, her repeated absences from home, her indifference to the gang for which she had once been so zealous, and added to these her desperate impatience to leave home that night at a particular hour. . . What was she up to?

Fagin was up early the next morning, and waited impatiently for the appearance of Noah, who after a delay that seemed interminable presented himself and started to eat a hearty breakfast.

"Noah," said Fagin, drawing up a chair and seating himself opposite.

"What's the matter?" asked Noah. "Don't yer ask me to do anything till I have done eating."

"You can talk as you eat, can't you?" asked Fagin, cursing Noah's greediness. Fagin leaned over the table. "I want you to do a piece of work for me, my dear, that needs great care and caution."

"Don't yer go shoving me into danger, or sending me to any more o' yer police officers."

"There's not the smallest danger in it, not the very smallest," said Fagin. "It's only to follow a woman."

"Who is she?"

"One of us."

"Oh!" cried Noah, curling up his nose. "Yer doubtful of 'er, are yer?"

"She has found some new friends, my dear, and I must know who they are," replied Fagin.

"I see," said Noah. "Where is she? Where am I to wait for her?"

"All that, my dear, you shall hear from me. I'll point her out at the proper time," said Fagin. "You keep ready, and leave the rest to me."

That night, and the next, and the next again, Noah sat ready. Six nights passed, and on each Fagin came home with a disappointed face, and briefly intimated that it was not time yet. On the seventh he returned earlier, and with an exultation he could not conceal. It was Sunday.

"She goes out tonight," said Fagin, "and on the right errand, I am sure, for she has been alone all day, and the man who would stop her going will not be back much before daybreak. Come with me. Quick!"

Noah started up and they left the house stealthily. Hurrying through a labyrinth of streets, they arrived at the public house Noah recognized as the one where he had first met Fagin.

It was past eleven o'clock, and the door was closed. It opened softly on its hinges as Fagin gave a low whistle. They entered, without a sound, and the door was closed behind them.

Scarcely venturing to whisper, Fagin pointed out a pane of glass to Noah, and signed to him to climb up and observe the person in the adjoining room.

"Is that the woman?" whispered Noah.

Fagin nodded yes.

Noah hastily descended, as the room door opened, and the girl came out. Fagin drew him behind a small partition which was curtained off, and they held their breaths as she passed within a few feet of their hiding place. After she had gone, Noah darted out behind her.

By the light of the lamps Noah saw Nancy's retreating figure, already at some distance before him. He advanced as near as he considered prudent, and kept on the opposite side of the street, the better to observe her motions. She looked nervously around two, three times, and then continued on her way.

The church clocks chimed quarter to midnight as two figures emerged on London Bridge. Nancy walked quickly, looking eagerly about her. Noah slunk along behind in the deepest shadow he could find. At nearly the centre of the bridge Nancy stopped. Noah stopped too.

A mist hung over the river, deepening the red glare of the fires that burnt upon the small boats moored off the different wharfs. The old smoke-stained storehouses on either side rose heavy and dull from the dense mass of roofs. The tower of old Saint Saviour's Church and the spire of Saint Magnus were visible in the gloom, but the forest of shipping below the bridge was nearly hidden from sight.

Nancy had taken a few restless steps to and fro, when the mighty bell of Saint Paul's tolled twelve. The hour had not struck two minutes, when a young lady accompanied by a grey-haired gentleman alighted from a carriage within a short distance of the bridge, and having dismissed the vehicle, walked straight towards it. They had scarcely set foot upon it, when Nancy started, and immediately made towards them.

As soon as Rose and Mr Brownlow saw Nancy, they stopped with an exclamation of surprise, but suppressed it immediately. A man in countryman's clothes came close up, and brushed against them.

"Not here," said Nancy hurriedly. "I am afraid to speak to you here. Come away, out of the public road, down the steps over there!"

As she uttered these words, the countryman looked around, and roughly asking what they took up the whole pavement for, passed on.

The steps to which Nancy had pointed were the landing stairs from the river. To these the countryman hastened, unobserved, and began to descend until he was hidden behind the pillar at the bottom. Soon afterwards he heard voices above him.

"This is far enough," said a voice, which was evidently the gentleman's. "For

He was hidden behind the pillar. Soon afterwards he heard voices above him.

what purpose can you have brought us to this strange place? Why not have let me speak to you above there, where it is light?"

"I was afraid to speak to you there," replied Nancy.

"And why did you not come last Sunday night?" asked the gentleman.

"I couldn't come," replied Nancy. "I was kept by force."

"By whom?"

"Him that I told the young lady of before. It's not very easy for me to leave him unless he knows why. I couldn't have seen the lady when I did if I had not given him a drink of laudanum before I came away."

"Did he awake before you returned?"

"No, and neither he nor any of them suspect me."

"Good," said the gentleman. "Now listen to me. This young lady has told me what you told her nearly a fortnight ago. To prove to you that I trust you, I tell you without reserve that we propose to extort the secret, whatever it may be, from this man Monks. But if he cannot be caught, or if we cannot find the secret from him, you must deliver up Fagin."

"I will not do it!" cried Nancy. "Devil that he is, I will never do that."

"Tell me why?"

"Bad life as he has led, I have led a bad life too. I will not betray one who has never betrayed me."

"Then," said the gentleman, "put Monks into my hands, and leave him to me to deal with."

"Monks would never learn how you came to be informed?" asked Nancy after a short pause.

"Never," said the gentleman.

Nancy then proceeded – in a voice so low that it was often difficult for Noah to hear what she said – to describe the public house that Monks frequented, and the night and the time when he was mostly likely to arrive. She paused a moment, to remember his features and appearance.

"He is tall," she went on, "but not stout. He has a lurking walk, and as he walks, constantly looks over his shoulder, first on one side, and then on the other. His eyes are sunk in his head so much deeper than any other man's that you might almost tell him by that alone. His face is dark, like his hair and eyes, and although he can't be more than six or eight and twenty, he is withered and haggard. Upon his throat, so high that you can see part of it, there is. . ."

"A broad red mark, like a burn or scald?" cried the gentleman.

"How's this?" said Nancy. "You know him!"

Rose uttered a cry of surprise, and for a few moments they were so still that Noah could distinctly hear them breathe.

"I think I do," said the gentleman. "We shall see. Now, you have given us most valuable assistance, young woman. What can I do to help you?"

"Nothing," said Nancy. "Let us part. I shall be watched or seen. Go! Go! All I ask is that you leave me, and let me go my way alone."

The gentleman turned with a sigh.

"This purse!" cried Rose. "Take it for my sake!"

"No!" replied Nancy. "I have not done this for money. And yet, give me something that you have worn. Your gloves, or your handkerchief, anything that I can keep as having belonged to you. There! Bless you! Good night! Good night!"

Rose Maylie lingered, but the old gentleman drew her arm through his and led her away. As they disappeared, Nancy sank down on the stairs and wept. After a time she arose and climbed to the street. The astonished Noah remained motionless for some minutes afterwards. When he had ascertained that he was again alone, he crept slowly out from his hiding place. When he reached the top of the stairs, he peeped out once more to make sure that he was unobserved, and then darted away to Fagin's house as fast as his legs would carry him.

CHAPTER 12

It was two hours before daybreak. Fagin sat in his room, his face pale, his eyes red and bloodshot. He crouched over the cold hearth, wrapped in an old coverlet, with his face turned towards a wasting candle that stood upon a table by his side.

Stretched upon a mattress on the floor lay Noah Claypole, fast asleep. Fagin glanced at him for an instant, then turned again to the candle. He was filled with hatred for the girl who had dared to mix with strangers, and with a fear for himself, a fear of detection, and ruin, and death. He sat without changing his attitude in the least, until he heard footsteps in the street.

"At last," he muttered, wiping his dry mouth. "At last!"

The bell rang gently as he spoke. It was Sikes.

"There!" said Sikes as he came in to the room and laid a bundle on the table. "Take care of that. It's been trouble enough to get it. I thought I should have been here three hours ago."

Fagin laid his hand upon the bundle, and locking it in the cupboard, sat down again without speaking. But he did not take his eyes off the robber, and now as they sat opposite each other face to face, he looked so fixedly at him that Sikes started back.

"Wot now?" he asked. "Wot do you look at me like that for?"

Fagin raised his right hand, and shook his trembling forefinger in the air, but his passion was so great that the power of speech was for the moment gone.

"Speak, will you!" said Sikes. "Or if you don't, it shall be because I've strangled you. Out with it!"

Fagin looked hard at the robber, and motioning him to be silent, stooped over the mattress on the floor and shook Noah to wake him. Sikes leaned forward in his chair, looking on with his hands on his knees, wondering what was to happen next.

"Noah! Poor lad!" said Fagin, looking up and speaking slowly with marked emphasis. "He's tired, tired with watching for *her* so long, watching for *her*, Bill."

"What d'you mean?" asked Sikes, drawing back.

Fagin made no answer, but bending over Noah again, hauled him into a sitting position. Noah rubbed his eyes, and giving a heavy yawn, looked sleepily about him.

"Tell me that again, about *Nancy*," said Fagin, clutching Sikes by the wrist as if to prevent his leaving the house before he had heard enough.

"You followed her?"

"Yes."

"To London Bridge?"

"Yes."

"Where she met two people?"

"So she did."

"A gentleman and a lady that she had gone to of her own accord before, who asked her to give up all her friends, and Monks first, which she did – and to describe him, which she did – and to tell her what house it was that we meet at, and go to, which she did – and where it could be best watched from, which she did – and what time the people went there, which she did. She did all this. She told it all, did she not?" cried Fagin, half mad with fury.

"That's just what she said," answered Noah.

"What did they say about last Sunday?"

"They asked her why she didn't come, last Sunday, as she promised. She said she couldn't."

"Why? Why? Tell him that."

"Because she was forcibly kept at home by Bill, the man she had told them of before," replied Noah. "She said that she couldn't get very easily out of doors unless he knew where she was going to, and so the first time she went to see the lady, she – ha! ha! ha! it made me laugh when she said it – she gave him a drink of laudanum."

"Hell's fire!" cried Sikes, breaking fiercely from Fagin. "Let me go!"

Flinging Fagin from him, he rushed from the room.

"Bill! Bill!" cried Fagin, following him. "You won't be. . . too. . . violent, will you, Bill?"

Sikes made no reply, but pulling open the street door, dashed out. Without a pause, without turning his head to the right or the left, or raising his eyes to the sky, or lowering them to the ground, but looking straight before him, the robber held on his course until he reached his own door. He opened it softly, with the key, and strode lightly up the stairs. He entered his own room, double-locked the door, and lifting a heavy table against it, drew back the curtain of the bed.

Nancy was lying half dressed, upon it. She raised herself with a startled look.

"Get up!" said Sikes.

"It *is* you, Bill!" said the girl with an expression of pleasure at his return.

There was a candle burning, but Sikes hastily drew it from the candlestick and hurled it under the grate. Seeing the faint light of dawn outside, Nancy got up to pull the curtain.

"Let it be," said Sikes, thrusting his hand before her. "There's light enough for what I've got to do."

"Bill," said Nancy in a voice of alarm. "Why do you look like that at me?"

The robber sat staring at her for a few seconds, with heaving breast, and then, grasping her by the head and throat, dragged her into the middle of the room, and looking once towards the door, placed his heavy hand on her mouth.

"Bill! Bill!" gasped the girl, struggling. "I won't scream or cry. Hear me! Speak to me! Tell me what I have done!"

"You know! You were watched last night. Every word you said was heard!"

"Then spare my life, as I spared yours," replied Nancy, clinging to him. "Bill, dear Bill, you cannot have the heart to kill me. I have been true to you, upon my soul I have!"

Sikes struggled violently to release his arms, but Nancy's were clasped around his, and pull as he would, he could not tear them away. He gave one hard wrench, freed an arm, and grasped his pistol. He knew if he fired, he would be heard immediately, so he beat it twice with all the force he could summon, upon the upturned face that almost touched his own.

Nancy staggered and fell, nearly blinded with the blood that poured from a deep gash in her forehead. Raising herself with difficulty on her knees, she drew out a white handkerchief, Rose Maylie's, and holding it up in her folded hands, breathed a prayer for mercy.

The murderer staggered backwards to the wall, and shutting out the sight with his hand, seized a heavy club and struck her down.

* * *

Sikes sat motionless for a long while. He had been afraid to stir. There had been a moan and a motion of the hand, and with terror added to rage, he had struck and struck again. Once he threw a rug over it, but it was worst to imagine the eyes, and imagine them moving towards him, than to see them glaring upwards. He plucked the rug off again.

He struck a light, kindled a fire, and thrust the club into it. He washed himself, and rubbed his clothes; there were spots that would not be removed, but he cut the pieces out, and burned them.

Such preparations completed, he moved backwards towards the door, dragging the dog with him. He shut the door softly, locked it, took the key, and left the house.

115

For two days, Sikes wandered until he thought of a safe place to hide. The dog, though. If any descriptions of him were out, it would not be forgotten that the dog was missing, and had probably gone with him. He resolved to drown him and walked on, looking about for a pond, picking up a heavy stone and tying it to his handkerchief as he went.

The animal looked up into his master's face. Whether his instinct told him something was in the making, or whether the robber's look was sterner than usual, he skulked a little farther behind than normal. When his master halted at the edge of a pool, and looked around to call him, he stopped outright.

"Come here!" said Sikes.

The animal came, but as Sikes stooped to attach the handkerchief to his throat, he growled and jumped away.

"Come back!" said Sikes.

The dog wagged its tail, but did not move. Sikes called him again.

The dog came forward, retreated, paused an instant, turned, and ran away at his hardest speed.

Sikes whistled again and again, and sat down and waited. But Bull's-eye did not appear, and at length Sikes resumed his journey.

CHAPTER 13

The twilight was beginning to close in when Mr Brownlow alighted from a carriage at his own door, and knocked softly. The door being opened, a sturdy man got out of the coach and stationed himself on one side of the steps, while another man dismounted too and stood upon the other side. At a sign from Mr Brownlow, they helped out a third man, and taking him between them, hurried him into the house. This man was Monks.

They walked up the stairs without speaking, and Mr Brownlow led the way into a back room. At the door of this apartment, Monks, who had ascended with reluctance, stopped. The two men looked to the old gentleman as if for instructions.

"He knows the alternative," said Mr Brownlow. "If he hesitates, drag him into the street, call for the aid of the police, and have him arrested as a felon."

"How dare you say this of me?" asked Monks. "By what authority am I kidnapped in the street, and brought here?"

"By mine," replied Mr Brownlow. "If you complain, I say again, throw yourself for protection on the law. If you wish me to charge you publicly, and consign you to a punishment I can see but cannot control, you know the way. If not, seat yourself in that chair."

Monks looked at the old gentleman anxiously, but reading nothing in his face but severity and determination, walked into the room, and shrugging his shoulders, sat down.

"Lock the door on the outside," said Mr Brownlow to the attendants, "and come when I ring."

"This is fine treatment," said Monks, "from my father's oldest friend."

"It is because I was your father's oldest friend, young man," replied Mr Brownlow, "that I am treating you gently now, yes, Edward Leeford, even now."

"What do you want with me?"

"You have a brother," said Mr Brownlow, "a brother the whisper of whose name in your ear when I came behind you in the street was, in itself, almost enough to make you accompany me hither, in wonder and alarm."

"I have no brother," replied Monks. "You know I was an only child."

"Listen to what I do know," said Mr Brownlow. "I shall interest you by and by. I know that of the unhappy marriage into which family pride forced your unhappy father, you were the sole child. But I also know the misery of that marriage. I know how indifference gave place to dislike, dislike to hate, and hate to loathing, until they separated. Your mother forgot it soon, but it rusted at your father's heart for years."

"And what of that?" asked Monks.

"When they had been separated for some time," returned Mr Brownlow, "and your mother, wholly given up to life abroad, had forgotten the young husband ten years her junior, he lingered on at home, and fell among new friends.

"These new friends were a retired naval officer, whose wife had died some half a year before, and two daughters, one a beautiful girl of nineteen, the other a child of two or three years old. As the old officer came to know your father, he grew to love him. His eldest daughter did the same. By the end of the year the girl was carrying their child."

118

"Your tale is of the longest," observed Monks, moving restlessly in his chair.

"At length," continued Mr Brownlow without seeming to hear the interruption, "your father was called to Rome to attend to a wealthy relative. The relative died, leaving him money. But he fell ill there. He was followed by your mother, who brought you with her. He died the day after her arrival, apparently leaving no will, so that the whole property fell to her and you."

Mr Brownlow paused and wiped his hot face and hands. "Before he went abroad," he continued more slowly, "he came to me."

"I never heard of that," interrupted Monks in disagreeable surprise.

"He came to me, and left me with a picture, a portrait painted by himself of the poor girl. He also confided in me his intention to sell his property, and after settling a portion on his wife and you, to flee the country with the girl. He would not say more, and that was the last time I saw him.

"I tried to find the girl and her family, but they had left their home. Why, none can tell. When your brother, a ragged, neglected child, was rescued by me by chance. . ."

"What?" cried Monks.

"I told you I should interest you before long. When he was rescued by me, his strong resemblance to this picture I have spoken of struck me with astonishment."

"You – you – cannot prove anything against me," stammered Monks. "I defy you to do it!"

"We shall see," replied Mr Brownlow. "I lost the boy. Your mother being dead, I knew that you alone could solve the mystery if anybody could, and as I had last heard that you were in the West Indies, I made the voyage. You had left, and were supposed to be in London. I returned, but could not find you. Within the last fortnight I have learned the whole story. You have a brother; you know it, and you know him. There was a will, as it turned out, which your mother destroyed, leaving the secret to you on her death. It contained a reference to some child, the child of your father and the poor girl – a child which you accidentally encountered. You went to the place of his birth. There existed proofs of his birth

119

and parentage. Those proofs were destroyed by you and now, in your own words to your accomplice, Fagin, 'the only proofs of the boy's identity lie at the bottom of the river, and the old woman that received them from the mother is in her coffin.'"

"No, no, no!" the coward declared.

"Every word," cried the old gentleman, "every word that has passed between you and this villain is known to me. Now, will you tell the whole truth?"

Monks was left with no choice. "Yes," he muttered.

"Set your hand to a statement, and swear to it before witnesses?"

"That I promise too."

"You must also make restitution to an innocent child. You have not forgotten the provisions of the will. Carry them into execution as far as your brother is concerned, and then go where you please."

Monks was considering this last demand, when suddenly the door was hurriedly unlocked and Dr Losberne entered the room in great agitation.

"The man will be taken," he cried. "He will be taken tonight!"

"The murderer?" asked Mr Brownlow.

"Yes, yes. His dog has been seen lurking about some old haunt, and there seems little doubt that his master is there or soon will be, under cover of darkness. A reward of a hundred pounds is proclaimed by government tonight."

"I will give fifty more," said Mr Brownlow, "and proclaim it myself upon the spot, if I can reach it. But Fagin. What of him?"

"When I last heard, he had not been taken, but he will be."

"Have you made up your mind?" asked Mr Brownlow, in a low voice, of Monks.

"Yes," he replied. "You will be secret with me?"

"I will. Stay here until I return. It is your only hope of safety."

They left the room, and the door was again locked.

* * *

Near to that part of the Thames in east London where the buildings on the banks are dirtiest and the boats on the river blackest with the dust of coal

120

and the smoke of close-built low-roofed houses, there is a place called Jacob's Island. It is surrounded by a muddy ditch, six or eight feet deep and fifteen or twenty wide when the tide is in, known as Folly Ditch. On Jacob's Island the warehouses are roofless and empty; the walls are crumbling down, the windows are windows no more, the doors are falling into the

streets, the chimneys are blackened. The houses have no owners; they are broken open and entered upon by those who have the courage or who strongly desire a secret residence.

In an upper room of one of these houses there were three men who, looking at each other every now and then, sat for some time in gloomy silence. One of these was Toby Crackit; the others, two companion robbers.

"When was Fagin taken, then?" Crackit asked the first robber.

"Just at dinnertime."

"What's come of young Charley Bates?" demanded the second.

"He hung about, not to come over here before dark, but he'll be here soon," answered the first. "There's nowhere else to go now, for the people at The Three Cripples are all in custody."

"The courts are in session," the second robber continued. "If they get the inquest over and Claypole turns King's evidence, as of course he will, they can prove Fagin an accessory before the fact, and have the trial on Friday, and he'll hang in six days."

"You should have heard the people groan," said the first. "The officers fought like devils, or the crowd would have torn him away. He was down once, but they made a ring around him, and fought their way along. You should have seen how he looked all about him, all muddy and bleeding, and clung to them as if they were his dearest friends. I can see the people jumping up, one behind another, snarling at him."

The robber pressed his hands upon his ears and got up and paced to and fro, like one distracted. While he was thus engaged, and the other two sat by in silence with their eyes fixed upon the floor, a pattering noise was heard on the stairs, and Bull's-eye bounded into the room.

"What's the meaning of this?" asked Toby Crackit. "He can't be coming here. I – I – hope not."

"If he was coming here, he'd have come with the dog," said the first robber, stooping down to examine the animal, who lay panting on the floor. "Here, give us some water for him; he's run himself faint."

"He's drunk it all up, every drop," said the second, after watching the dog some time in silence. "Covered with mud, lame, he must have come a long way."

"But how comes he here without the other?" asked Crackit.

"He must have got out of the country, and left the dog behind. Given them the slip somehow," replied the first robber.

This solution, appearing the most probable one, was adopted as the right; the dog, creeping under a chair, coiled himself up to sleep.

It now being dark, a candle was lighted and placed upon the table. The three men sat, speaking little, and then only in whispers, when suddenly a hurried knocking was heard at the door below.

"Charley Bates," said the first robber.

The knocking came again. "No," said Crackit. "He never knocks like that."

Crackit went to the window, and shaking all over, drew in his head. There was no need to tell them who it was; his pale face was enough. The dog, too, was on the alert in an instant, and ran whining to the door.

"We must let him in," said Crackit. "There's no help for it."

Crackit went down to the door, and returned followed by a man with the lower part of his face buried in a handkerchief, and another tied over his head under his hat. He drew them slowly off. Blanched face, sunken eyes, hollow cheeks, beard of three days' growth; it was the very ghost of Sikes.

He laid his hand upon a chair which stood in the middle of the room, dragged it back close to the wall, and sat down.

Not a word was exchanged. He looked from one to the other in silence. When his hollow voice broke silence, they all three started. They seemed never to have heard its tones before.

"How came that dog here?" he asked.

"Alone. Three hours ago."

"Tonight's paper says that Fagin's took. Is it true, or a lie?"

"True."

They were silent again.

Sikes carried his eyes slowly up the wall behind him, and said, "Is. . . is. . . the body buried?"

They shook their heads.

"Why isn't it!" he retorted with the same glance behind him. "What do they keep such ugly things above the ground for?. . . Who's that knocking?"

Crackit left the room and directly came back with Charley Bates behind him. Sikes sat opposite the door, so that the moment the boy entered the room, he saw the ghastly figure.

"Toby," said the boy, falling back as Sikes looked at him, "why didn't you tell me *he* was here?"

"Charley!" said Sikes, stepping forward. "Don't you – don't you know me?"

"Don't come nearer me," answered the boy, still retreating, and looking with horror in his eyes upon the murderer's face. "You monster!"

The man stopped halfway, and they looked at each other; but Sikes's eyes sank gradually to the ground.

"Witness you three," cried the boy shaking his clenched fist, and becoming more and more excited as he spoke. "Witness you three, I'm not afraid of him. If they come here after him, I'll give him up, I will. He may kill me for it if he likes, or if he dares, but if I am here, I'll give him up. I'd give him up if he was to be boiled alive. Murder! Help! Murder! Help! Down with him!"

Pouring out these cries, and accompanying them with violent gesticulation, the boy threw himself, single-handed, upon the murderer, and in the intensity of his energy and the suddenness of his surprise, brought Sikes heavily to the ground.

The three spectators seemed quite stupefied. The boy and man rolled on the ground together, but the contest was too unequal to last. Sikes had Charley down, and his knee was on his throat. Suddenly Crackit pulled him back with a look of alarm, and pointed to the window. There were lights gleaming below, voices, the tramp of hurried footsteps. The gleam of lights increased; the footsteps came more thickly and noisily on. Then came a loud knocking at the door.

"Help!" shrieked Charley. "He's here! Break down the door!"

"In the King's name," cried the voices outside, and the hoarse cry arose from the crowd.

"Break down the door!" screamed Charley. "Run straight to the room where the light is. Break down the door!"

Strokes, thick and heavy, rattled upon the door and lower window-shutters.

"Open the door of some place where I can lock this screeching boy," cried Sikes fiercely, running to and fro, and dragging the boy now as easily as if he were an empty sack. "That door! Quick!" He flung Charley in, bolted it, and turned the key. "Is the downstairs door locked fast?"

"Double-locked and chained," replied Crackit.

"The panels, are they strong?"

"Lined with sheet iron."

"And the windows too?"

"Yes, and the windows."

"Do your worst!" cried the desperate ruffian, throwing up the window and menacing the crowd. "I'll cheat you yet!"

The crowd yelled louder than ever. Some shouted to those who were nearest to set the house on fire; others roared to the police officers to shoot him dead. Some called for ladders, some for sledgehammers; some ran with torches looking for the murderer; and all waved to and fro in the darkness and joined from time to time in one loud, furious roar.

"The tide," cried the murderer as he staggered back into the room and shut the faces out. "The tide was in as I came up. Give me a rope, a long rope. They're all in front. I may drop into the Folly Ditch, and clear off that way. Give me a rope!"

The panic-stricken men pointed to where such articles were kept; the murderer, hastily selecting the longest and strongest rope, hurried to the housetop.

All the windows in the rear of the house had been long ago bricked up, except one small trap in the room where Charley was locked, and that was too small even for the passage of his slight body. But through it he had shouted to those outside to guard the back; and thus, when the murderer emerged at last on the housetop by the door in the roof, a loud shout proclaimed the fact to those in front, who immediately began to pour around.

Sikes planted a board firmly against the door so that it could not be opened from the inside; and creeping over the tiles, looked over the low parapet.

The water was out, and the ditch a bed of mud.

The crowd had been hushed during these few moments, watching his movements. The minute they perceived he was defeated, they raised the loudest cry of all.

"They have him now!" cried a man on the nearest bridge.

"I will give fifty pounds," cried an old gentleman from the same bridge, "to the man who takes him alive. I will remain here, till he comes to ask me for it."

There was another roar. At this moment the word was passed among the crowd that the door was forced at last. They turned, and poured back around to the front of the house.

Sikes had shrunk down, defeated by the ferocity of the crowd, and the impossibility of escape; but seeing this sudden change, sprang to his feet, determined to make one last effort for his life by dropping into the ditch, and at the risk of being taken, trying to creep away in the darkness and confusion.

He set his foot against the chimney, fastened one end of the rope tightly and firmly around it, and with the other made a strong running noose. He could let himself down by the rope to within jumping distance of the ground, and had his knife ready in his hand to cut it and then drop.

At the very instant when he brought the loop over his head before slipping it under his armpits, and when the old gentleman shouted to those near him that the man was about to lower himself down, Sikes's foot slipped. He threw his arms above his head, dropped his knife and uttered a yell of terror.

He tumbled over the parapet. The noose was on his neck. It ran up with his weight, tight as a bowstring. There was a sudden jerk, and there he hung. The murderer swung lifeless against the wall.

A dog, which had lain hidden till now, ran backward and forward on the parapet with a dismal howl, and collecting himself for a spring, jumped for the dead man's shoulders. Missing his aim, he fell into the ditch, turning over as he went. He died as soon as he struck the ground.

There was a sudden jerk, and there he hung.

CHAPTER 14

Two days after Sikes's death Oliver was in a carriage rolling fast towards his native town. Mrs Maylie, Rose, Mrs Bedwin and Dr Losberne were with him; Mr Brownlow followed in another carriage, accompanied by Monks.

As they approached the town, and at length drove through its narrow streets, Oliver became increasingly excited. There was Sowerberry's the undertaker's just as it used to be, only smaller and less imposing than he remembered it; there were all the well-known shops and houses; there was the workhouse, with its dismal windows frowning on the street.

They drove straight to the door of the chief hotel, and there was Mr Grimwig, all ready to receive them. There was dinner prepared, and there were bedrooms ready, and everything was arranged as if by magic.

Notwithstanding all this, when the hurry of the first half-hour was over, a silence fell on the party. Mr Brownlow did not join them at dinner, but remained in a separate room. The two other gentlemen hurried in and out with anxious faces. Once Mrs Maylie was called away, and after being absent for nearly an hour, returned with eyes swollen with weeping. All these things made Rose and Oliver nervous and uncomfortable.

At length, when nine o'clock had come, and they began to think they were to hear no more that night, Dr Losberne and Mr Grimwig entered the room, followed by Mr Brownlow and a man whom Oliver almost shrieked with terror to see, for it was the same man he had seen looking in with Fagin at the window of his little room. Then they told Oliver the man was his brother. Monks cast a look of hate at the astonished boy, and sat down near the door. Mr Brownlow, who had papers in his hand, walked to a table near which Rose and Oliver were seated.

"This is a painful task," said Mr Brownlow, "but these declarations must be repeated here. We must hear them from your own lips."

"Go on," said Monks. "Quick. I have done enough. Don't keep me here."

"This child," said Mr Brownlow, drawing Oliver to him, "is your half-brother; the illegitimate son of your father, my dear friend Edwin Leeford, by poor young Agnes Fleming, who died in giving him birth."

"Yes," said Monks, scowling at the trembling boy. "You have the story there." He pointed impatiently to the papers.

"I must have it here too," said Mr Brownlow, looking around upon his listeners.

"Listen then! His father – my father – was taken ill in Rome and was joined by his wife, my mother. He died the day after we arrived. Among the papers in his desk were two addressed to you," he turned to Mr Brownlow, "and accompanied by a short note to you with instructions that the papers should not be forwarded until after he was dead. One of these papers was a letter to Agnes; the other a will."

"What of the letter?" asked Mr Brownlow.

"The letter was a confession. He reminded her of the day he had given her the little locket and the ring with her Christian name engraved upon it, and a blank left for the surname which he hoped one day to have given her."

"The will," said Mr Brownlow.

Monks was silent.

"The will," said Mr Brownlow, "left you and your mother each a sum of eight hundred pounds. The bulk of his property he divided into two equal portions, one for Agnes Fleming, and the other for their child."

"My mother," said Monks, "burned this will. The letter never reached its destination, but she kept it and the other proofs in case Agnes's family ever tried to lie away the blot. She told the girl's father the truth, and goaded by shame and dishonour, he fled with his children, changing his name so that his friends might never find him. A short while afterwards he was found dead in his bed. The girl had left her home, in secret, some weeks before. He had searched for her, and it was on the night when he returned home, assured that she was dead, that his old heart broke.

"My mother bequeathed these secrets to me on her deathbed. She would not believe that the girl was dead, but was filled with the impression that a boy had been born, and was alive. I swore to her, if ever he crossed my path, to hunt him down. She was right. He came my way at last. I began well, and but for gossip, would have finished as I began!"

Mr Brownlow turned to the group, and explained that Fagin, who had been Monks's accomplice, had a large reward for keeping Oliver ensnared.

"The locket and the ring?" asked Mr Brownlow, turning to Monks.

"I bought them from the man and woman I told you of, who stole them from the nurse, who stole them from the dead woman," answered Monks.

Mr Brownlow nodded to Mr Grimwig, who disappeared quickly and shortly returned, pushing in Mrs Bumble and dragging her unwilling husband behind him.

"Do my hi's deceive me!" cried Mr Bumble. "Or is that little Oliver? Oh, O-li-ver, if you know'd how I've been a-grieving for you. . ."

"Hold your tongue, fool," murmured Mrs Bumble.

"How do you do, sir," said Mr Bumble, turning to Mr Brownlow. "I hope you are very well."

Ignoring the remark, Mr Brownlow stepped up to the couple and asked as he pointed to Monks, "Do you know that person?"

"No," replied Mrs Bumble.

"Perhaps *you* don't?" said Mr Brownlow, addressing her husband.

"I never saw him in all my life," said Mr Bumble.

"Nor sold him anything, perhaps?"

"No," replied Mrs Bumble.

"You never had, perhaps, a certain gold locket and ring?" said Mr Brownlow.

"Certainly not," replied Mrs Bumble.

Again Mr Brownlow nodded to Mr Grimwig, and again Mr Grimwig left the room, returning with two pale old women from the workhouse.

"You shut the door the night old Mrs Thingummy died," said the first, pointing at Mrs Bumble. "But you couldn't shut out the sound, nor stop up the chinks in the wall."

"We heard her try to tell you what she'd done, and saw you take the paper from her hand, and watched you too, next day, at the pawnbroker's shop," said the other.

"I *did* sell them, and they're where you'll never get them. So what now?" snapped Mrs Bumble.

"Nothing," said Mr Brownlow, "except that neither of you will be employed in a situation of trust again. You may leave the room."

"It was all Mrs Bumble. She *would* do it," said Mr Bumble, looking around to make sure his wife had left.

"That is no excuse," said Mr Brownlow. "You were present when the jewellery was destroyed, and indeed are the more guilty of the two, in the eye of the law, for the law supposes that your wife acts under your direction."

"If the law supposes that," said Mr Bumble, squeezing his hat emphatically in both hands, "the law is a ass – a idiot. If that's the eye of the law, the law is a bachelor; and the worst I wish the law is, that his eye may be opened by experience – by experience."

With that Mr Bumble fixed his hat on very tight, and putting his hands in his pockets, followed his wife down the stairs.

"Young lady," said Mr Brownlow turning to Rose, "give me your hand." Turning to Monks he said, "Do you know this young lady, sir?"

"Yes," replied Monks.

"I never saw you before," said Rose faintly.

"The father of Agnes had two daughters," said Mr Brownlow. "What happened to the other – the child?"

"The child," replied Monks, "when her father died was taken in by some poor cottagers, who reared it as their own."

"Go on," said Mr Brownlow, indicating to Mrs Maylie to approach. "Go on!"

"The child led a miserable existence until a widow lady saw the girl by chance, pitied her, and took her home. She remained there and was happy. I lost sight of her, two or three years ago, and saw her no more until a few months back."

"Do you see her now?"

"Yes. Leaning on your arm."

Rose almost fainted, but Oliver ran to her and threw his arms around her. "My mother's sister!" he cried. "But I can never call you aunt. You will always be my own dear sister!"

CHAPTER 15

The court was lined, from floor to roof, with human faces. All looks were fixed upon one man – Fagin. He stood there, with one hand resting on the wooden slab before him, the other held to his ear, and his head thrust forward to enable him to catch every word that fell from the judge, who was delivering his charge to the jury. Fagin had scarcely moved since the trial began, and now that the judge had ceased to speak, he still remained in the same strained attitude of close attention.

There was a slight bustle in the court. Looking around, Fagin saw that the jurymen had turned together to consider their verdict. Then a deathlike stillness came again, and Fagin saw that the jurymen had turned towards the judge. Hush!

They only sought permission to retire.

He looked wistfully into their faces, one by one, when they passed out, as though to see which way the greater number leaned; but it was fruitless. The jailer touched him on the shoulder. He followed mechanically to the end of the dock, and sat down on a chair.

He looked up into the gallery again. Some of the people were eating, and some fanning themselves with handkerchiefs, for the crowded place was very hot. There was one young man, sitting nearby, sketching his face in a little notebook. He wondered whether it was like him, and looked on when the artist broke his pencil point and made another with his knife, as any idle spectator might have done.

He fell to counting the iron spikes before him, and wondering how the head of one had been broken off, and whether they would mend it, or leave it as it was. Then he thought of all the horrors of the gallows and the scaffold, and stopped, then went on to think again.

At length there was a cry of silence, and a breathless look from all towards the door. The jury returned. Perfect stillness ensued. Not a rustle. Not a breath. The verdict was announced. *Guilty.*

The building rang with a tremendous shout, and another, and another, and then it echoed loud groans, like angry thunder. It was the crowd outside, greeting the news that he would die on Monday.

The noise subsided and he was asked if he had anything to say why sentence of death should not be passed upon him. He only muttered that he was an old man, an old man, an old man, and so, dropping into a whisper, was silent again.

They led him through a paved room under the court, through a gloomy passage and into one of the condemned cells, where he was left, alone.

He sat down on a stone bench opposite the door and tried to collect his thoughts. They gradually fell into their proper places, so that in a time he had the whole, almost as it was delivered. To be hanged by the neck, till he was dead – that was the end. To be hanged by the neck till he was dead.

Then came night – dark, dismal, silent night. The boom of every church bell came laden with one, deep, hollow sound – Death.

The day passed off. Day? There was no day; it was gone as soon as come, and night came on again.

Saturday night came. He had only one more night to live. And as he thought of this, the day broke – Sunday.

He cowered upon his stone bed, and thought of the past. He had been wounded with some missiles from the crowd on the day of his capture, and his

134

He had only one more night to live.

head was bandaged with a linen cloth. His red hair clung to his face; his beard was ragged and twisted into knots; his eyes shone with a terrible light.

The space before the prison was cleared, and a few strong barriers, painted black, had already been thrown across the road to break the pressure of the expected crowd, when Mr Brownlow and Oliver appeared at the gate, and presented an order of admission to the prisoner. They were immediately admitted and followed the jailer to the cell.

Fagin was seated on the bed, rocking himself from side to side. His mind was wandering to his old life, and he was muttering.

Mr Brownlow advanced towards him. "You have some papers," he said, "which were placed in your hands by a man called Monks."

"It's a lie altogether," replied Fagin. "I haven't one – not one."

"For the love of God," said Mr Brownlow solemnly, "do not say that now, upon the verge of death. Tell me where they are."

"Oliver," cried Fagin, beckoning to him. "Here, here! Let me whisper to you!"

"I am not afraid," said Oliver as he let go of Mr Brownlow's hand.

"The papers," said Fagin, drawing Oliver towards him, "are in a canvas bag, in a hole a little way up the chimney in the front room."

"Have you nothing else to ask him?" inquired the jailer.

"No other question," replied Mr Brownlow.

The door of the cell opened. Fagin, who had hold of Oliver, pushed him forward. "Press on, press on!" he cried. "Faster, faster!"

The jailer laid hands on him, and disengaging him from Oliver, held him back. He struggled for a minute and then sent up a cry that rang through the thick walls of the prison, and rang in their ears until they reached the yard.

Day was dawning when they emerged. A great crowd had already assembled, the windows were filled with people, pushing, quarrelling, joking. Everything told of life, but one dark cluster of objects in the centre of all – the black stage, the cross-beam, the rope, all the hideous apparatus of death.

AND LAST

The fortunes of those who have figured in this tale are simple to tell. It appeared, on investigation, that if the property remaining in the custody of Monks were equally divided between himself and Oliver, it would give to each a little more than three thousand pounds. By the provisions of his father's will, Oliver would have been entitled to the whole, but Mr Brownlow, unwilling to deprive Monks of the opportunity of pursuing an honest career, proposed the division, to which Oliver agreed.

Monks retired with his share to a distant part of America where, having quickly squandered it, he once more fell into his former ways and died in prison.

Mr and Mrs Bumble, deprived of their positions, were gradually reduced to poverty and finally became paupers in the very same workhouse in which they had once lorded over others.

Noah Claypole received a free pardon from the Crown in consequence of being admitted approver against Fagin. After some consideration, he went into business as an Informer.

Charley Bates, appalled by Sikes's crime, decided that an honest life, after all, was the best. He struggled hard but succeeded in the end and became the merriest young shepherd in all Northamptonshire.

Mrs Maylie and Rose returned to their home together, attended by Giles and Brittles.

Mr Brownlow adopted Oliver as his son and moved with him and Mrs Bedwin to within a mile of Rose and Mrs Maylie. Dr Losberne moved to a cottage in the neighbourhood, where he was often visited by Mr Grimwig, who had become a firm friend.

By the altar of the old village church there stands a white marble tablet, which bears one word: "Agnes," in memory of the mother of one boy, Oliver Twist.

Charles Dickens was born in Portsmouth on 7 February 1812. He was one of eight children of John Dickens, a clerk in the Navy Pay Office. In 1821 John Dickens lost his job with the Navy and the family moved to London so that he could look for work. But in 1824 he was arrested for debt and sent to prison with his entire family, apart from the young Charles. The boy was now twelve, old enough to earn a living, and was sent to work in a blacking factory. For six shillings (thirty pence) a week he had to stick labels on bottles of paste-blacking, a substance used to colour leather or metal. Charles never forgot how unhappy he was at this time. He hated the work; he also had to walk the four miles home on his own, and was alone at night.

His father was released from prison after three months and Charles was reunited with his family. He left the blacking factory and for the next three years went to school. Then in 1827, when he was fifteen, he began work as an office boy in a solicitor's office. Meanwhile, his father had become a reporter for the *Morning Herald* newspaper and Charles decided that he, too, would try to be a journalist. He taught himself shorthand and went to study every day in the British Museum. In 1828 he became a reporter of debates at the House of Commons for the *Morning Chronicle*.

Five years later, using the name "Boz", he started to write short, humorous pieces for the *Monthly Magazine*. These were collected together and published as *Sketches by Boz* in 1836. In the same year, he started to write another series of pieces, *The Pickwick Papers*, which were very popular and established his fame as a writer. He also married. Over the next fifteen years he and his wife Catherine were to have ten children – seven boys and three girls.

In 1837 Dickens began to write *Oliver Twist*. It was first published in short parts in the monthly magazine *Bentley's Miscellany* from February 1837 until April 1839. It was not published in book form until November 1838.

The story was inspired by Dickens' sympathy for the very poor, especially children, and the hard lives they led, and also by his own memories of being poor as a child. In the early 1800s wages were very low and the money paid by the government to help the poorest was not enough to help everyone. The poor went to workhouses like the one Oliver was born in because it was the only place where they could find food and shelter. The workhouses were often badly run, dirty and always overcrowded.

In 1834 the government passed a new law to try to improve conditions for the poor. The government thought that, if possible, the poor should find work, and not rely on the workhouses for shelter. The new law therefore made life in the workhouses even more uncomfortable than before to show the poor that they would be better off if they supported themselves. Under the new law food was strictly rationed: in one workhouse the diet for each person was one and a half pints of gruel – a thin mixture of oatmeal boiled in water – a day, and on Fridays, apart from the gruel, three slices of bread, half a bowl of rice pudding and a small piece of cheese. When, in the story, Oliver left Mrs Mann, he was brought back to a workhouse governed by the new law. It is not surprising that he asked for "more". The new law said nothing about allowing the poor in the workhouse to go out for fresh air or exercise, and their work, such as unpicking old rope as Oliver is made to do, was boring and unproductive.

The government's plan failed. Poor people who tried to support themselves often could not find work, or earned too little to feed themselves and their families. They returned to the workhouses, where life was even harder than before the new law was passed. In Dickens' story Oliver escaped, only to fall into the clutches of Fagin and his gang. Criminals such as these would also have existed in the 1800s. And so would characters such as Mr Brownlow, with whom

Oliver at last finds a happy home. Few children actually born in the workhouse were so lucky.

After *Oliver Twist* Dickens continued to write book after book up until his death over thirty years later. He also travelled, visiting the United States, Canada, Switzerland, Italy and France.

Nicholas Nickleby, Dickens' first novel after *Oliver Twist*, was published in 1839; then came *American Notes* in 1842 and *Martin Chuzzlewit* in 1843. That year, too, *A Christmas Carol* was published. This famous story was the first of Dickens' Christmas stories, which he continued later with *The Chimes* and *The Cricket on the Hearth*. He reached the height of his fame in 1850 with *David Copperfield*, which is the most autobiographical of his novels. After this came *Bleak House* in 1852–3, *Hard Times* in 1854, and *Little Dorrit* between 1855 and 1857. Dickens also gave public readings, both in England and the United States, and wrote speeches, letters, plays and articles for magazines. His last three most important novels were *A Tale of Two Cities*, published in 1859, *Great Expectations*, published in 1861, and finally *Our Mutual Friend*, written between 1864 and 1865. By the middle of the 1860s his health was failing and his last novel, *The Mystery of Edwin Drood*, was never completed. He died on 9 June 1870 and was buried in Poets' Corner, Westminster Abbey.

ACKNOWLEDGEMENTS

Christian Birmingham would like to thank the following for their help in his
historical research for the illustrations in this book:
The Police Staff College, Bramshill
The Museum of London Picture Library
The Guildhall Library, London
Westminster Reference Library, London.

He is also grateful to the following people for their help and support:
Marcus, Ricky, Nick, Gordon, Dai, Megan, John, Daniel, Tim,
Michael and Rosemary.